COWHOUSE CREEK SHOWDOWN

Cowhouse Creek Showdown

COL. R.C. HARTJEN

This book is dedicated to Captain Anthony Wayne Horton, CSA, and to his great granddaughter, Irene Smith Hartjen (1940-2015), my much-loved wife who was always supportive in all my endeavors.

Contents

About the Author

Chapter 1

A cold, wet wind struck the tall man who emerged from a carriage in front of the War Department. Washington, at the best of times, smelled like swamp, wet horse manure, and rotting garbage. Now, at the end of October 1865, the unpleasantness of the city was further compounded by thousands of demobilized soldiers, freedmen and women, and the rest of the chaotic aftermath of the Civil War.

Brevet Major General Seth Wolfgang Horton, nicknamed "Wolf" by his West Point classmates in a natural response to his mother's attempt to preserve a bit of Hessian heritage, adjusted his hat and sword before attempting to walk up the steps leading to the building's entrance. In the closing days of the war, shrapnel from an exploding rebel shell had all but severed his right leg at mid-thigh, consigning him to weeks of fever, infection, and, finally, slow recovery. Before he reached the door, he began to seriously question the wisdom of his decision to leave behind the cane he had used for support after he had finally begun to walk again.

As he entered the building, the sound of the cold wind was replaced by the noise and confusion of the overcrowded room. Clerks, civilians, and officers all seemed to be hurrying to accomplish the various tasks that kept the War Department running. Horton found himself being jostled along a corridor until finally a fat major spotted him and came to his rescue.

"General Horton?" he inquired. Upon receipt of an affirmative nod, the major said, "Please come with me, sir. General Sheridan is expecting you. I hope you will excuse the conditions here. Sometimes it seems as if every officer who ever served under General Sheridan is trying to find active service on the frontier, and at his old rank, too."

The last part of the comment was not lost on Horton. It had been little more than five years ago that he had been a newly promoted captain serving with Colonel Bob Lee's Second Cavalry Regiment in Texas. The promotions he had won since then on the field of battle were all temporary. Theoretically, Horton knew, he could leave this meeting today wearing two silver bars instead of the two silver stars he now wore. Had the war not come, Horton would still have had about fifteen years to wait before promotion to major. Try as he might, Horton could not generate much concern over the uncertainty of his career. About the only concern he could muster was over the possibility of becoming a captain again and having to work for this upstart major, who clearly had spent the war fighting his battles in the bowels of the Washington bureaucracy. Horton dismissed this possibility almost immediately. He had made his decision. After today, he, not the Army, would control his life.

"Here we are, sir. Go right in. The general is expecting you." The major disappeared into the background.

Horton removed his hat and twitched his uniform into a more presentable appearance. His clothes fit poorly because of the weight he lost during his long recovery from the wound. He reminded himself that the uniform only had to make do for the next hour or two.

He could do nothing about the pallor caused by his long hospitalization. Horton looked like what he was: a man who had been through the hell of more than four years of continuous warfare and had barely lived to talk about it. He knocked on the door and, hearing the command to enter, stepped through the doorway.

General Sheridan presented quite a contrast to Horton. Short when compared to Horton's more than six-foot, three-inch frame; and bearded, it was sometimes difficult to picture this man as the great cavalry commander he had proven himself to be. He greeted Horton warmly.

"Come in, Wolf. Have a seat. Can I interest you in a drink or a cigar? No? Well, it's good to see you again, boy. There were times last April and May when I thought I wouldn't."

Horton shook the general's hand and sank gratefully into a chair. His leg was really giving him hell.

"There were times along then when I didn't think you would either, sir. I'm pleased to report that we were both wrong."

Sheridan's smile widened into a grin. "So we were, Wolf, so we were. Somehow, I don't mind being wrong in this case. It's good to have you back."

"It's good to be here, sir, but I'm afraid that I have an unpleasant duty to perform. I have come today to offer my resignation in person. I know that this is a poor way to repay the support you have given me over the years, but it's something I must do."

"Now Wolf, I don't want you to be hasty." Sheridan rose from his own chair and moved closer to Horton. "You were the best damned commander I had, and the Army can't afford to lose you. Hell, boy, I can't afford to lose you. With the Army being cut back to a fraction of its size, the best we have been able to do for you is the command of a regiment. I have no doubt that you will wear stars again someday. We need commanders with experience on the frontier. This country is moving, Wolf, and it's moving west. Rebels who lost everything in the war, our soldiers who have nothing to return to, adventurers, speculators, and immigrants—Wolf, all of them are headed west to find a dream. What they are going to find is hunger, dust, hard work, and hostile Indians. It's only men like you who can keep all of that from turning into a bloodbath that would make Gettysburg look like a tea party."

"Thank you for your confidence, sir, but I doubt that I'm up to the task. On a campaign I probably wouldn't last an hour in the saddle. I'm tired, sir, just about worn out. I've been at war either on the frontier or during the rebellion since I graduated from the Academy in '54. I've seen enough blood to float a frigate. I agree that this country is going to expand westward and that means more war, this time with every Indian west of the Missouri. To tell you the truth, a good bit of my sympathy lies with them. They've been lied to and cheated since the first white man set foot on the continent, and our greed will see to it that it continues."

"I understand what you're saying, Wolf, but the fact remains that we need you in command of a regiment. All your training and experience can't be replaced easily. Your duty is out west, commanding troops."

"I also have a duty to my family in Texas, General. I haven't seen them since I left there with Pleasanton and the rest of the Union Cavalry in '61. I heard that my four brothers all went off with Hood and his brigade, but I have heard nothing about my parents. I need to go home to find out what's left of the family and help put things back together again. I really must insist that you accept my resignation, sir."

Sheridan's face clouded. "Horton, one of the nice things about being senior is that I don't have to do a damned thing I don't want to. Now I'm going to tell you what's going to happen."

Angry now, Sheridan walked to his desk, sorted through some papers, and, selecting one, turned back to Horton, who had gotten to his feet.

"I've got here in my hand your commission as a colonel. You will accept it. Half of the damned brevet generals in the Army would give their right arms for it. Pleasanton, you know, was offered a majority and turned it down; Custer took a lieutenant colonelcy.

"You will proceed to New Orleans and determine the status of the investigation into allegations of corruption, fraud, and theft that's going on right now. You will send a written report directly to me. When you have finished that task, I'll have the surgeon place you on recuperation leave for a period of one year from the date of the report you render. At the end of that time, you will assume the duties of commanding officer of the cavalry regiment stationed at Ft. Riley, Kansas. Should you not report at that time, for whatever reason, I will then accept this resignation, but not one damned minute before!"

Sheridan's anger moderated somewhat. "You can, of course, try going over my head. I hope you won't do that, boy. I'm betting that once things are put right at home, you'll need the Army as much as it needs you."

Horton paused a moment before responding. He had seen Sheridan angry many times, but never before had that anger been direct at him. *What the hell,* he thought, *maybe he's right. I might not be able to take off the uniform as easily as I thought.*

"I understand, General, and I accept your conditions. I cannot promise you that I will change my mind about resigning, but I will think it over carefully."

"I know you will, Wolf, and I trust you to make the right decision. My written orders will be delivered to you at your hotel this afternoon. By the way, it might interest you to know that while you were in the hospital, that renegade colonel of yours, Donovan, I think his name is, managed to finesse a captaincy and is commanding a troop at Riley. I'm not sure that Kansas is ready for both of you. Now get out of here so I can get some work done."

Horton picked up his hat and shook the offered hand. "Thank you for your patience, General. I'm sorry to have added to your concerns. I appreciate all that you have done for me. I really do."

"Just make damned sure you don't let me down now, Wolf. there is too much work yet to be done."

Horton made his way out of the building and down the steps to the street. While he had been inside, it had started to rain, making the day even more unpleasant. Limping badly now, Horton finally located a cab and returned to his lodgings.

He had been lucky to find the room, and had he not had someone searching for one before he was ready to leave the hospital, he might not have found one at all. The room itself was small and plain, located on the second floor of a hotel showing the ravages of the war

years when occupant turnover was high and mainte-
nance all but non-existent.

When he entered, Horton found the room to be
cold, damp, and dingy. Lighting the lamp, he mused
over how he had been outmaneuvered by Sheridan. It
was only later, after his trunks had been packed and
the final preparations had been made for his trip, that
Horton realized the real purpose of his mission in New
Orleans. The crusty old bastard does have a heart after
all, he thought. He wants to reduce the amount of leave
I have to use returning home, not to have me check up
on an investigation. I wonder what other tricks he has
up his sleeve.

Chapter 2

"Ten-HUT!" bellowed the sergeant major as Colonel Horton walked through the doorway of the military headquarters in New Orleans. The sergeant major had come quickly to brace, but he could not keep the smile from his face. From his manner it was clear that he knew Horton from somewhere, and Horton searched his memory for a name to go with the face.

"At ease, Sergeant Major," Horton said as the man's name suddenly came to him "It's good to see you again, Flynn. How long has it been?" he asked as he stuck out his hand in greeting.

"At least five years, General Horton, sir. We served in the old Second Cavalry together, sir, before the late unpleasantness. It's surprised I am that you'd be rememberin' me, sir, with me bein' on a trooper at the time." The sergeant major shook his hand self-consciously after first wiping his own on his trouser leg as if to cleanse it before touching an officer.

"Nonsense, Flynn. A man always remembers good troopers and bad officers. I'm pleased to see those stripes on your sleeves. You deserved them years ago."

"Thank you, sir. Thank you. It was the war that got me the stripes, but happy I'd be to be just a trooper again an' do without the war, General."

"I know what you mean. I feel the same way about it. And it's "colonel' now, not 'general.' I know that most officers go by their brevet rank, but I prefer to be addressed by the rank I get paid for. In my opinion, it's time to stop living in the past and get on with doing the job now."

"And right you are, too, General—I mean, Colonel, sir," Flynn said admiringly. "Now, himself in there," he said, nodding towards the door marked Commanding Officer, "he insists on bein' addressed as 'General.' An' if you'll be pardonin' me for sayin' it, the man wouldn't be makin' a pimple on a good trooper's ass ... er, backside, beggin' the Colonel's pardon."

Horton chocked back a laugh and cleared his throat instead. "Would you tell the major that I'd like to see him? And while I'm in there, please keep everybody else out of here. I don't want this conversation to become common knowledge."

"Not to worry, sir. I'll be guardin' the door myself. If that's all, sir, I'll be seein' if himself is up to receivin' visitors today." When Horton nodded, the sergeant major did a smart about-face, marched to the commanding officer's door, knocked once, and entered without waiting for a command to enter. He emerged a moment later and stood at attention next to the doorway as he announced, "The commander will be seein' you know, sir."

As Horton walked by him, the sergeant major gave him a wink and closed the door, leaving the two officers alone.

"Come in, Colonel," said the figure behind the desk on the far side of the room. "I'm General Tuttle. What can I do for you?"

Horton stopped and looked at the man. He was a balding man in his mid-forties who might have once been an imposing figure, but who had long since gone to fat. His seamed face was covered with ruptured blood vessels, and his eyes were red and watery. His whole appearance suggested years of heavy drinking and personal neglect.

"I know who you are, Major," Horton said coldly. "The first thing you can do is to stand at attention when a senior officer comes into the room. You're not a general any longer."

Tuttle got slowly to his feet and buttoned his tunic at the throat. His West Point class ring glittered as he completed the task. He stared sullenly at Horton for a moment, then said, "Whatever you say, sir, but if this had been a year or two ago, I'd ...."

"If this had been a year or two ago, Major," Horton interrupted, "you'd still be standing at attention for me while I decided whether to have you court-martialed or simply cashiered from the Army. You see, Tuttle, I know all about you. I know that you commanded a brigade at Manassas Creek. It broke and ran after the first volley. I can understand that; the troops were untrained and had never heard a shot fired at them before. What I can't understand is why it took you a week longer than it took your troops to find your way back to the unit. Looking at you now, I suspect that you crawled into a bottle and stayed there. If Washington could have proved that they'd have had you shot. Instead, they relieved you of command and sent you off to command a series of detachments that administered the affairs of captured cities. You kept your star but never commanded in the field again."

Tuttle's mouth dropped open, then snapped shut. "How do you know all this?" he asked angrily. "I've a good mind to call you out, sir!" he exclaimed indignantly.

"Don't bother. I'm the man they sent to put your old brigade back together when you ran out on it. I know that you're all mouth and no action. You know why I'm here now. You also know who sent me. Suppose you stop posturing and tell me what the status is of the investigation into the allegations of graft and corruption in the administration of this city?"

Tuttle clenched and unclenched his fists several times before he seemed to gain control of his anger, then said, "The investigators left yesterday. I'm sure that General Sheridan will have the report later this week. I was completely exonerated. It was all the doing of my executive officer, a Captain of Volunteers named Jackson Devereaux."

"Where can I find him?" Horton asked.

"How should I know?" Tuttle responded. "I can't be expected to be responsible for everybody. As far as I know, he deserted as soon as word got out that an inspector was coming out from Washington."

"And just when was that?"

"About two months ago."

"Did you notify anyone that he had deserted?"

"No, I didn't. You see, he didn't actually desert, at least not technically. He left a letter of resignation on my adjutant's desk. It was only later that we discovered that he was behind all the trouble here."

Horton thought for a minute. "What have you done about rounding up any of his accomplices? He must have had some help from others in the city."

Tuttle flushed even redder than he had before. "Damn you, Horton. Damn you and your superior than thou attitude. How dare you judge me? Why I was a captain when you were a plebe at West Point. I've had every dirty job the Army has had to offer while you got all the breaks. The only reason that you're wearing those eagles now is because of all your politicking with Sheridan. Now you're here to cheat me out of my retirement. Well, to hell with you and all of your boot-licking kind. I have nothing more to say to any of you."

Horton stood there and watched spittle run down the major's chin. His cold glare seemed to whittle away at what remained of the older man's composure. Soon Tuttle began to sob silently, all trace of defiance gone. Horton continued to watch as he opened a desk drawer, removed a bottle, and took a long drink.

Horton walked over to the major and took the bottle gently from his hand. Tuttle offered no resistance but sat down in his chair and rested his head in his hands. Horton walked to the door and called over Sergeant Major Flynn.

"Sergeant Major, I want you to have the major escorted back to his quarters and placed under guard. As of this moment, he's relieved of his duties and under house arrest. Have his quarters searched and remove all alcohol. I also want you to send in the next ranking officer. Do you have any questions about what I want?"

"No, sir, I don't," Flynn said as a grin creased his craggy face. "And a fine day it is for the Army, too, I'm thinkin'. It's an action long overdue, if the Colonel'd be wantin' my opinion."

"Well, I don't Sergeant Major. And for your information, it's a sad day for the Army when an officer who has devoted so much of his life to the service of his country has to be removed from office. If I find that you had any part in his fall, you'll follow him into arrest!" Horton snapped. "Now carry out my orders without any more of your comments!"

The sergeant major snapped to attention and saluted. "Yes, sir," he said crisply. "And sorry I am that I troubled the colonel with my thoughtless words. It'll not happen again, I assure you," he said, then did an about-face and marched off in search of the second-in-command and some guards. Horton's harsh words had stung him, and he cursed himself for foolishly presuming on an old friendship by voicing his unsolicited opinions. Now, when it was too late, he remembered that Horton never would tolerate any criticism of an officer by an enlisted man, regardless of the circumstance. For that matter, he had never allowed troopers to criticize a corporal or sergeant, either. "He's a great one for discipline," he said to himself as he hurried on his way. "And God help us; we need it around here!"

Horton stood at the door and waited for the sergeant major to return with the guards. Once Major Tuttle had been escorted from the building, Horton sat down behind the desk and started going through the drawers. Aside from another whiskey bottle and a dirty glass, the desk contained only old newspapers, a book or two, and some yellowed directives. As he slid the last drawer shut, a knock on the door caused him to look up. Before he could answer, the sergeant major stepped into the room and announced the arrival of Captain Kimberlin, the adjutant.

The officer who marched into the office and halted in front of Horton was of average height, sandy-haired, and thin to the point of illness. The officer held his salute until Horton returned it, then stood at attention until Horton told him to sit down in the chair next to the desk.

Horton looked at Kimberlin for a minute before he formed an impression of the man. In contrast to the new shoulder straps which indicated that the officer was a Captain of Cavalry, the uniform was well-worn and showed signs of having been neatly patched on more than one occasion. The captain was clean-shaven and clear-eyed, both of which were in pleasant contrast to the major who had just left the office. Horton decided that he was prepared to like the man.

"I see that your uniform has seen a lot more service than your shoulder straps have," Horton said conversationally. "Have you just been promoted?"

"Yes, sir, I guess that you could say that," Kimberlin said in a voice surprisingly deep for a man of his size. "I mustered out at the end of the war and only came back in about three months ago. I was fortunate enough to get this rank. I thought that I was going to go to a cavalry regiment, but I got orders assigning me here, instead."

"And how do you like the duty?" Horton asked.

"I don't, sir, to be honest about it. I came back in the Army because I'd grown to love the cavalry, and the Army gave me a desk instead. If I'd have wanted a desk, I would have stayed a schoolteacher."

"Have you served long in the cavalry?"

"I served throughout the war in the First Iowa. I had the honor to command it at the end. There may have been better regiments in the Union Army, but I never saw any," he said with pride.

Horton laughed and said, "You sound like every other cavalryman in the Army. We all think we served in the best regiment there was. I don't think that I'd have much use for anyone who didn't think that way. I take it that you're the senior officer here now."

"After Major Tuttle, yes, sir. The former second-in-command would have been, of course, but it seems that he was deeply involved in the matters that were recently under investigation and departed somewhat hurriedly."

"Major Tuttle has been relieved of his duties. You will take command until Washington sends a replacement for him. What I'd like to hear from you is your impression of what went on around here."

Captain Kimberlin squirmed uncomfortably in his chair. "I don't know how much help I can give you, Colonel. I really wasn't here that long before the scandal broke. All I know I told to the other investigators. I'd be happy to give you a copy of the report and answer any specific questions that you might have."

"It sounds to me like you might have something to hide," Horton said in a hard voice. "Or are you trying to cover up for someone?"

"Neither one, sir. It's just that the major was my commander and I don't like to say anything behind his back."

"Loyalty is a grand thing, Captain," Horton said evenly, "but in this instance I think that loyalty to the Army takes precedence over loyalty to a friend."

"The major is no friend of mine," Kimberlin said. "In fact, if he has his way, I'll be out of the Army again soon. You see, sir, it was me that suggested to the city authorities that they contact the War Department about all the corruption here. I was unable to convince the major that we really had a big problem. Of course, he blamed me for the investigation. He felt that I was to blame for stirring up a mess. I just did what I thought was right, sir," he said miserably.

Horton thought about what the officer had just said. "Would you do the same thing again?" he finally asked.

"I'd like to think that I would, sir, but I honestly don't know. I've been under house arrest since word come that there was going to be an investigation."

"Well, you're not under arrest any longer, and I think that your behavior has been honorable. Bring me the record of the investigation and give me a chance to read it. When I'm done, we'll discuss it," Horton said.

Captain Kimberlin stood up, saluted, and left the office in search of the record. He returned in a few minutes with the documents in one hand and a cup of coffee in the other. He placed both in front of Horton and quietly withdrew.

Horton read the report through carefully twice, then left the building for lunch. He returned to the office around two o'clock and spent the rest of the day making notes of questions he wanted to ask the captain. When he had finished, he gave the report to the sergeant major and left word for Captain Kimberlin to report to him the next morning. Horton then went to his hotel, where he spent a sleepless night thinking about the case.

Captain Kimberlin was waiting for Horton when the latter entered the building at eight o'clock the next morning. The sergeant major had fresh coffee waiting and saw to it that both officers were comfortably situated before he withdrew to his own office.

Horton and Kimberlin went over the case, point by point, until Horton was satisfied that he had learned all that he ever would of the facts surrounding the investigation. It was clear that the culprit had indeed been Captain Jackson Devereaux, "Delta Jack" to his cronies, an unscrupulous officer of uncertain background who had organized all the vice in New Orleans. In addition to that, he had initiated a series of licensing requirements for legitimate businesses. A license had become necessary for nearly any transaction, and one could only be obtained from Jack Devereaux. Both Horton and the investigators determined that Devereaux had stolen close to half a million dollars with this scam before he had fled the city, taking most of his henchmen with him.

Finally, Horton pushed back his chair and stretched. "Well, Captain, I guess that's all I need to know. I'll finish up my report to General Sheridan and tell him what I found here. I'm also going to ask him to order you to the cavalry regiment at Fort Riely. Before I leave, I'll give you a letter of introduction to Captain Donovan, who is commanding a troop there. He'll see to it that you get a job to your liking. Don't let that big Irishman lead you astray, now. He's a smooth-talking devil who could charm the rattles off a snake."

Captain Kimberlin was speechless. Finally, he found his tongue and managed to ask, "Why are you doing this for me?" He added hastily, "Don't get me wrong, sir, I appreciate it, I really do. I do wonder how the commander is going to feel about me showing up on his doorstep, so to speak."

Horton laughed. "Actually," he said, "the commander asked for you by name. There will be no trouble over whether you're welcome or not. Just see to it that you soldier hard when you get there."

Kimberlin stood up and saluted in preparation for leaving. His face was wreathed in a smile. "You can bet that I will, sir. By the way, who is the commander?" he asked, almost as an afterthought.

"A real hardnose named Horton. Now get out of here. I've still got a report to write. Send in the sergeant major on your way out."

The captain closed the door behind him and stared off into the distance, as if he were in a daze. The sound of Flynn's footsteps snapped him back to the present.

"What's the matter, Captain?" Flynn asked innocently. "Did the colonel give you the very devil, did he?"

"As a matter of fact, he gave me a job. Is he always that hard to figure out?"

Flynn nodded and smiled. "That he is, sir," he said. "And you'll not be makin' the trip alone. Himself is sendin' me along to keep you out of trouble, and maybe that Captain Donovan as well. Did the colonel want anything else?"

"Oh, yes. He said to send you in. I nearly forgot. I seem to be losing my grip today."

Flynn laughed and knocked on the door. This time he waited until he heard Horton tell him to enter.

"Sergeant Major," Horton said after the door was closed, "I want you to bring Major Tuttle over here in an hour. You're to leave the guards in the outer office, but I want you in here, too. It's my intention to offer the major some options, and I'll need you for a witness."

"Yes, sir," Flynn answered, "the colonel can count on me, and I'll see to it that nobody else knows what's said."

Horton nodded in dismissal, and the sergeant major retired from the room.

An hour later, Flynn returned with Major Tuttle. Horton told Tuttle to be seated, then got down to business.

"Major, I've finished my job here. I'm satisfied that the investigators did their jobs well. I am also confident that you played no active part in this plan to extort money from the citizens of this city. I do, however, believe that you were negligent in allowing this scam to operate right under your nose, and you were derelict in your duty when you refused to listen when Captain Kimberlin brought the matter to your attention, or tried to, anyway. In addition to that, you are guilty of being drunk on duty and being disrespectful towards a superior officer. It is my intention to offer you a choice: you may either resign right now from the Army, or you can stand court-martial for the offenses I have just mentioned. The choice is yours; you have one minute to decide."

Tuttle looked at Horton, desperate to see a sign that the latter was only trying to scare him. The only thing that Tuttle saw in Horton's eyes was an end to his career.

"Damn you, sir. You leave me no choice at all. Can't you give me another chance? After all, we both graduated from the same school, even if we aren't classmates. I need a break, sir. You owe me that much."

"I have already given you a break by offering you a choice. You had your last break when some classmate let you stay in the Army after Manassas Creek. I do, however, owe the troops better leadership than you have ever been able to provide. I refuse to stick them with you any longer."

"Bur, sir! What about my retirement?" Tuttle wailed.

"You've been retired for years. That's enough. From now on, you will have to do something useful for a living or starve to death. I really don't care which. Now, which will it be: the resignation or the court-martial?"

Tears welled in Tuttle's eyes as he reached for the pen and signed the resignation that Horton had prepared for him. He slammed the pen down when he finished and looked defiantly at Horton.

"I won't give you the satisfaction of watching me starve to death. Someday I'm going to see you ruined, Horton, just like you've ruined me. I swear it!"

"You've ruined yourself, Tuttle, and I get no satisfaction from forcing you out. Personally, I don't think you can stay sober enough to cause me any trouble."

Tuttle started to say something else, but Horton cut him off. "I've heard enough from you," he said. "Sergeant Major, have this man escorted off the post."

"Yes, sir!" snapped Flynn. "Come this way, Mister Tuttle, darlin'. It's time for you to be goin'."

Still muttering oaths and threats, Tuttle allowed himself to be led from the room. Horton gathered his things together and followed him out a few minutes later.

"I'll be seeing' you at Fort Riley, sir," Flynn said as he opened the front door for Horton.

"I hope so, Sergeant Major, but if things don't turn out well in Texas, I may resign myself. Whatever happens, look after the captains. They'll need you."

Flynn just nodded. He didn't know what was going on, but he damned sure wasn't going to stick his nose into the colonel's business.

Chapter 3

Six weeks later, Horton sat on his horse nearly two days' ride north of Austin. Darkness came early in mid-December, and Horton was trying to decide whether to find a suitable campsite or to press on to the Circle H ranch headquarters. He was tired and stiff from his ride, even though he had regained some of the weight and energy he had lost during his long hospital stay.

As inviting as a warm bed and a home-cooked meal were to a man who had experienced neither for a long time, his natural caution reinforced by years of warfare, made Horton extremely reluctant to approach the ranch headquarters unexpectedly after dark. His father always kept men around the house to guard against the threat from marauding Indians and renegade whites who drifted through the west seeking easy money and avoiding work. A bullet from the dark could not sort out friend from foe, as Stonewall Jackson and many of Horton's friends had discovered to their dismay during the war.

Horton was also uncertain about what he would find at the ranch. There was no guarantee that his family still controlled the more than one hundred sections of prime graze that ran along the north side of the Cowhouse Creek. Common sense demanded that the approach to the headquarters be made after daylight, when the risks from an accidental confrontation would be reduced.

Reluctantly, Horton resigned himself to another night in a cold camp. He decided to press on to the Cowhouse and make camp on the high ground to the north of it, on home range. He scanned the ground to his front and flanks from his vantage point in a cedar grove about halfway up a hill and picked out a route to the next major terrain feature.

He had learned as a youth that in this country, the shortest distance between two points was seldom a straight line. Some obstacle, human or otherwise, always seemed to thwart the man in a hurry. He had known this country well at one time, and little seemed to have changed. Horton knew that he was about two miles south of the Cowhouse. On the other side of the creek, some folks named Robinette had come to grief at the hands of raiding hostiles back in the '50s, and an overlook point there still was referred to by name.

Horton urged his horse forward and moved from one observation point to another by a route that was mostly concealed. He finally came to the creek just as the last of the light left the western sky. Although he was still a good three hours' ride from the ranch headquarters, Horton was filled with a sense of being home.

Quickly, he crossed the creek and, in a small grove of cedar and mesquite, built a small fire. He used the branches of a large cedar to break up what little smoke there was. He did not unsaddle his horse or remove any more than the minimum amount of gear he needed to prepare a quick meal of bacon, hard bread, and coffee. Horton knew that as small and protected as his fire was, it could still be seen. He had lived too long in the field to ever sleep close to a place where a fire had burned after dark. In this country, light could attract too many unwanted guests.

After he had eaten and cleaned his gear, Horton doused the fire and led his horse away from the creek. Mounting, he rode about a quarter of a mile upstream before moving north towards the foot of the bluff overlooking the valley. There, he found a good campsite that offered good grazing for his horse and that was out of the cold wind that had sprung up from the north. Horton unsaddled his horse and rubbed him down, then hobbled him before selecting his own sleeping place deep in the shadows of the bluff.

As he lay in his blankets waiting for sleep to come, he thought of New Orleans and the report he had just submitted to General Sheridan. Horton had found the investigation all but completed by the time he arrived. The conclusion drawn by the investigating officers was that a Captain of Volunteers named Jackson Devereaux had been the responsible person behind the graft, theft, and corruption that had been reported to

Sheridan. Known to his henchmen as "Delta Jack," Devereaux had deserted at the first hint of an investigation. No one seemed to know where he had gone and Horton had been unable to uncover any further leads.

Horton rolled over and forced all thoughts of New Orleans from his mind. He was very tired and slowly drifted off to sleep. He spent a quiet night there with only the sound of the wind and an occasional snort from his horse to break the silence.

An hour before dawn found Horton packed and ready to ride into the ranch headquarters. He had debated over whether to take the time to cook breakfast or ride directly to the ranch, and ended up compromising with a breakfast of a cold biscuit and water.

Horton inspected his weapons as daylight began to filter into the valley. This was a routine from which he never varied when he was in the field. He was armed exceptionally well for the day. He carried a model 1860 Henry repeating rifle that had been presented to him by his regiment when he left to command a division.

Horton carefully unloaded it, wiped the barrel and ammunition with an oily cloth, and reloaded. Although the rifle would hold twelve rounds, Horton had discovered that carrying the weapon fully loaded over long periods weakened the spring that forced cartridges into the action, creating malfunctions just when the weapon was needed most. Experience had taught him that ten rounds in the weapon was an acceptable compromise between available firepower and reliability.

Horton carried two pistols, both of which he wiped down and inspected. The first pistol was an 1860 Colt Army Model of .44 caliber. Early in the war, he had ordered a pair of these fine pistols directly from the Colt factory. He had disliked the grips on the standard 1860 Army model, and had ordered this pair with the older, smaller, but more comfortable 1851 Navy grips. He had also ordered the pistols fully engraved at the factory by the chief engraver, a man by the name of Wolfe, who signed his work with a wolf head engraved on the hammer of each pistol.

Most people who were aware of the pistols and not of his background assumed incorrectly that Horton got his nickname because of the pistols. These pistols had been further modified during Horton's stay in the hospital by adapting them to fire the .44 caliber Henry rimfire cartridge. Several men, including one named Richards, had devised conversion processes which allowed rapid reloading of metallic cartridges even when the shooter was mounted. The advantages of having a rifle and a pistol that fired the same ammunition were quickly recognized by Horton and he was glad that he had had both pistols converted. One he wore on the left side, butt forward, in a flapped holster. The mate to it was secured in his bedroll.

The second pistol that Horton carried was a Colt Model 1862 Police pocket pistol with a four-inch barrel in .36 caliber. This was the standard percussion cap model. When fully loaded, the cylinder contained five shots, but to make absolutely sure that the gun was safe, Horton loaded only four chambers and left the hammer resting on the empty one.

This pistol was Horton's emergency gun, his insurance, and he carried it at the small of his back beneath his belt, with the butt positioned so that the pistol could be drawn with his right hand. The pistol was difficult to draw when he was wearing heavy clothing, but Horton felt that if he ever needed the gun, speed would not be very important.

A three-inch blade pocketknife rounded out Horton's weaponry, although he considered the knife to be more a utility tool than a weapon. To him, an edged weapon was a cavalry saber. His was stored in a warehouse somewhere in New Orleans.

Horton mounted his horse and followed a steep path up the side of Robinette Pointe to the flat land above. The land was covered with mesquite and cedar, which made travel slow and limited visibility. As the sun rose higher and the chill in the air lessened, he moved into country that was gently rolling and more open. Horton automatically moved from hill to hill over the most concealed route, avoiding hill tops and large open areas. After an hour, he was able to unbutton his heavy coat; after another hour he removed it and tied it behind his saddle. It promised to be a warm day in central Texas and Horton was eager to get home.

Topping a rise, he looked out over a large valley split by a winding stream and studded by large live oak trees.

On the far side of the valley, the Circle H headquarters buildings could be seen. The main house was a long, single floor adobe and rock affair built along Spanish lines. Its tall ceilings and wide porches allowed for coolness in the summer but was hard to heat in the winter. A bunkhouse for the crew, two fair-sized rock and adobe barns, a large stone corral, and several small outbuildings made up the remainder of the ranch headquarters.

Horton felt a sudden surge of excitement as he started his horse down the rise towards the house. His instincts told him that something was wrong. The excitement of a moment ago was replaced by cautiousness as he wheeled his horse into a position from which he could observe the headquarters without being noticed.

He tried to identify what was wrong. There was nothing going on down there that would suggest danger. In fact, there was nothing moving anywhere around the headquarters. He knew that something should be going on at mid-morning. There should have been at least the signs of a fire in the house, but the whole place gave the impression of abandonment.

Horton took a pair of binoculars from his saddle bags and scrutinized the buildings more closely. The doors and gates were all closed, and the windows were unshuttered and intact. Not abandoned, he thought, just empty.

Horton replaced the binoculars and extracted the Henry from its scabbard. He positioned it across the pommel of his saddle with his thumb on the hammer and finger on the trigger. With his left hand, he reined his horse back to the trail and cautiously approached the headquarters.

Nothing moved as he stopped his horse a hundred yards from the house. The ground was open here, with little cover for a man on horseback or afoot. His father had built this place with defense in mind, and several times over the years, the soundness of that decision had been demonstrated. Horton believed that on many more occasions, the place had been left alone because it was easily defended. Standing in his stirrups, Horton shouted a "Hello" at the house. When nothing happened, he eased his horse forward cautiously.

As he drew abreast of the stone corral, a click of metal drew him up short. An old man with a raised rifle stepped into the gate opening to the right of Horton and said softly, "That's far enough, mister. Just sit real still and state your business."

Horton carefully turned his head to look at the man. It took him a moment to recognize him. Breathing a sigh of relief, he said, "It's me, Joe, Seth Horton. You can put that cannon away."

Joe Penbrook stared at Horton for a few moments and then, easing the hammer of the big Sharps forward, smiled and said, "Damned if'n it ain't. Git down offen that horse so I can see you. I thought you was dead."

Horton slid the Henry back into the scabbard and dismounted. Joe had come to Texas when Austin was still called Waterloo and had been the foreman of the Circle H since before Horton could remember. He was older, grayer than he remembered him, but it was plain that he was still capable of running things. Horton shook his hand warmly.

"Where is everybody, Joe?" Horton let his gaze sweep around him. "This place looks deserted."

"Let's go into the big house, Seth, an' I'll fix us some coffee, or what passes as such nowadays. It's a long story an' it'll be a long time in tellin', so we might as well get comfortable. Put your horse in the barn while I start a fire."

Horton nodded and led his horse to the barn. After unsaddling it and seeing that it had hay and water, he walked to the house and entered the kitchen. He found a fire roaring in the stove and Joe about to pour some concoction of doubtful origin into a coffee pot.

"Here, Joe. Use this. It's straight from New Orleans." Horton tossed him the small sack of coffee beans. Joe caught the sack and emptied part of it into the grinder, whirled the handle a few times, and dumped the results into the pot.

"Let's set," Joe suggested, and toed a chair towards Horton. "As you can see, everyone else is gone. There ain't no easy way of tellin' it, son, and I wasn't ever knowed to be no silver-tongued devil, so I'll just give it to you straight out. Your folks is both gone. Your ma passed on during the first year of the war. Just didn't wake up one mornin'. Your pa went last winter. He was comin' back from town and his horse fell with him. Horse showed up next mornin' an' me 'n' one of the boys started backtrackin'. Found him about nightfall. He was fair busted up but still breathin'. We brung him back here and nursed him best we could, but he commenced to coughin' hard, took a fever, an' died about two weeks later."

Horton was shaken. He supposed that something had happened when he first became aware that the ranch headquarters appeared deserted, but to hear of the loss of both of his parents at once was a blow that staggered him. Fighting down the lump in his throat, he turned back towards Joe.

"What about my brothers, Joe? Has there been any word of them? I heard they all rode off with Hood."

"That they did. Used to get letters here pretty regular—two, three a year for a while. James wrote that Enoch got killed near Little Roundtop at Gettysburg. I ain't heard from the other three for more than a year, closer to two. 'Course, we didn't hear nothin' from you neither, an' you turned up safe enough. I wouldn't write those other three off quite yet, was I you."

"Three gone at one telling," Horton thought, "and no word of the other three." He was numb from the shock of his loss. Clearing his throat and knuckling moisture from his eyes, Horton said, "I guess it's up to just us, at least for a while, Joe. If the boys are alive, they will be home sooner or later. Tell me the rest of it. Why does this place look like a ghost town?"

"Mostly the war, Seth. 'Bout all the young men, and middle-aged ones too, went off to fight damn Yanks. No offense, you understand."

Embarrassed, he continued, "Our hands wasn't no different. When the war got over, we was down to half a dozen hands. Mostly we was holdin' the herds together, what was left of 'em. Money was real scarce around here, and one or two of the boys drifted off when they heard of cash money jobs up to the north.

"Then along about last June, we started to have rustler problems, though why I don't know. Steers ain't worth the cost of movin' 'em these days. Anyway, we lost about half the herd durin' the hot months to rustlers. Sheriff couldn't or wouldn't do nuthin', an' we lost the trail when we tried. 'Bout three months ago, Jim Smiley—you remember him—an' old Pete Flanagan got themselves killed up at the north line shack. When one of 'em didn't come in for supplies, I went up there. The shack was in ashes an' Jim 'n' Pete were past the bad smellin' stage of bein' dead."

"Indians?" asked Horton.

"If they was, they wasn't like any I ever seen or heard about. Both Jim 'n' Pete was hangin' from a cottonwood, durned near dried like beef jerky. Their hands was tied and they had been shot to pieces. Naw, it wasn't no Indians. Somebody was tryin' to send a message, an' I guess he did, too, 'cause the last two hands lit out the night after I got back from buryin' them two. Night or so after that, the rest of the herd got run off. I tracked 'em 'till they split up. I followed one group an' lost 'em about a week east of here. Only stock left on the place is about a dozen horses and a bunch of stray steers, maybe two hundred all told."

"It doesn't sound good, Joe."

"We're fair broke, an' that's a fact. We ain't alone in that matter, neither. Everyone else around here is in that same fix, 'ceptin' maybe that fella Delacourte over to the Rafter T."

"Who's Delacourte? What happened to Thompson at Rafter?" Horton responded.

"Well, Thompson started losin' stock first around here right after the war. His hands all quit or got run off, and he got in a real bind for money. He borrowed some money from the bank, and that damn Yankee banker Delacourte started pushin' real hard for his money. When Thompson couldn't pay in gold or green-backs, Delacourte foreclosed and put Thompson off his land."

"Just who is this Delacourte?"

"Claims to have been some big Yankee officer. Calls hisself 'Colonel' and gets right huffy with them that don't. Came in from New Orleans 'long about last May. He seemed to have plenty of money and took to sur-roundin' hisself with every hard case he could find. When he hired up all the locals, he sent off for more. He's bought everything worth havin' that's for sale an' it seems that everything he wants goes up for sale sooner or later. He took over the bank, lock, stock, and barrel. Fact is, he's been out here a time or two, sniffin' around like a blind dog in a meat house. I happened to be pretty well forted up both times, an' he tamed down pretty good lookin' up the bore of that Sharps fifty. I expect he'll be back, though. Death, taxes, and Delacourte's got a lot in common."

Horton thought about what he had heard. Rustlers had been around since cows were invented. Taxes were nothing new, either, although before now they had been token payments. Real problems seemed to have started about the time that Delacourte showed up. Yet it could still be a coincidence. Vast change had taken place when the fighting had stopped. Almost anyone could be behind the trouble here. Still, Delacourte seemed to be the man who profited from the trouble and the situation at Circle H fit into the same pattern as those of the Rafter T and the others.

"Joe," asked Horton, "what's our situation with money? How much do we owe and are we getting any pressure for payment?

"Your pa borrowed money towards the end of the war. When Delacourte took over the bank, he took over all the markers, too, even your pa's. I took the last of the gold money your pa left in my keepin' an' paid the last interest payment. There's more due after the first of the year, and I'm real glad you're here to deal with that. I was plannin' on payin' 'em in lead."

"Is Benton still the county seat?"

Joe nodded.

"Then I'll ride in there tomorrow and find out what's going on. I'd like to see what we're up against. Any chance of finding some hands in town?"

Joe shook his head. "Delacourte's run out most of the good boys and hired all the hard cases. Comes to a fight, it'll probably be just me 'n' you against the lot of 'em. Them ain't good odds."

"You're right, Joe. I think Delacourte's going to need a lot more help than what he's got, judging by this way you've held him off up until now."

Joe exploded into laughter. "You may be right at that. With both of us here now, the poor man ain't got a chance. How do you reckon we ought to break the news to him?"

"I'll take care of that tomorrow. Right now, I'd like you to fill me in on everything else that's happened. While you're telling, I'll cook us up something to go along with that coffee."

The two men talked for the rest of the day. Horton went out to the barn just before dark, saddled his horse and rode west away from the ranch buildings. After he had gone about half a mile, he turned north and rode a wide circle around the buildings. On the ridge to the north of the house, he found a spot where a man had spent considerable time observing the buildings. One man, thought Horton. Several piles of manure indicated the spot where a horse had been hidden. "He must have seen me ride in." Dismounting, Horton examined the horse droppings. "Still warm," he muttered under his breath. "He must have seen me ride out, too."

As he rode back to the house, Horton couldn't help wondering who the observer was and why so much attention was being paid to the Circle H.

Chapter 4

Breakfast was finished by the time the sun put in its appearance over the hill. It had gotten colder during the night, and Horton had been glad to find a heavier coat that fit him among the clothing stored in the house. He had found a layer of ice on the trough when he watered the stock, and Horton mentally prepared himself for the ride to Benton. Fortunately, the wind had not picked up. It would be a cold ride, nevertheless.

Joe appeared from around the corner of a barn leading one of the Circle H horses. "Since you're the brand now, I figured you better ride one of the brand's horses. That sorrel you rode in here looks like he'd be a fair enough road horse, but you'd probably hurt his feelin's if you was to ask him to do any work. He probably don't even know how to break a sweat."

Horton looked over the horse. He was a big bay—sixteen hands at the shoulder, deep in the chest, and built for stamina. His eyes were wide, nostrils flared, and he gave the impression of walking on his tiptoes. He was a beauty, Horton decided.

"Look at him," said Joe. "You couldn't bust an egg under those hooves. From the tune he's whistling through his nose, you might find the first few miles a might entertainin'. 'Course, it won't take no time atall to go those miles, neither."

"How did you ever keep a horse like that?" asked Horton. "I know the Confederacy must have stripped the country of good horses during the war for cavalry remounts. I didn't see him in the barn, either."

"They did, they did. But your pa was thinkin' faster than they was an' held a small bunch back in the hills, enough to keep us in prime horseflesh while the other folks 'round here was lookin' for tame cows to ride or either bustin' their bones tryin' to catch and break some of them runty mustangs that was still around. Those scrubs in the barn was mostly for show. While you was putterin' around tryin' to take care of the stock, I fetched this one from up the valley a piece."

"Well, he's a great looking horse. I wish I'd been mounted half as well during the war. Has he got a name, Joe?"

"Far as I know, his name is 'Horse.' Bunch of damned foolishness, namin' horses, if you was to ask me. I never do. That way it don't bother me none if I ever have to eat 'em."

Unable to argue with that piece of logic, Horton helped Joe saddle the horse. After a moment or two of intense activity, the horse settled down enough to keep at least two feet on the ground and Horton turned towards town. After the first mile or two, the horse had quieted enough for Horton to draw the Henry from its scabbard and carry it resting on the pommel of his saddle.

The trail kept to open ground that offered few opportunities for trouble. After about ten miles, the trail widened into a road. Horton stayed alert for trouble. These were dangerous times for lone riders in Texas or anywhere else, for that matter. A man that arrived at his destination was a man who was observant and cautious along the way.

Benton was not a big town when compared to Washington, New Orleans, or even Austin. It did, however, boast of four streets, a courthouse, and a town square. In the fall of 1860, there had been one saloon, four stores, a livery, a bank, two farriers, a church, a school, one hotel, and one bawdy house. As he rode along the main street, Horton discovered that two of the stores had closed, the church had burned down, and two new saloons had been built. He was certain that other changes had been made as well.

The town was busy. Wagon and horse traffic were heavy, and around the saloons the people spilled from the boardwalks into the street. Few people paid any attention to Horton, although several eyed his horse closely. Animals such as that were not to be found just anywhere, and the rider who owned one was much envied.

Horton drew up in front of the bank, dismounted and hitched his horse to a rail. He was relieved to see that the horse stood calmly. Horton didn't think that the foreman would give him a horse that would cause him trouble, but he couldn't be sure. Sometimes Joe had a strange sense of humor. Cradling the Henry in the crook of his left arm, Horton entered the bank.

It took a minute or two for his eyes to adjust from the bright sunlight to the dim interior. Horton moved across the room to the cashier who was identified by a nameplate as Mr. Purdy. A small, thin man, perhaps fifty years old, Purdy was busily going over some ledgers when Horton stopped at the counter. Purdy did not take the time to look up until he had come to a convenient stopping place.

"Can I help you?" The tone of his voice suggested that Purdy doubted it, but that he was prepared to waste a moment or two by answering a dumb question or offering some other small service.

"I'm here to look into the debt situation for the Horton place, the Circle H," responded Horton.

"What business is it of yours?" Purdy asked icily.

"I'm Horton. Now, suppose you fetch the bill and I'll settle up."

Purdy looked around quickly as if to gather support and, finding none, brought a ledger over to the counter. He thumbed through the pages until he came to one designated for the Circle H.

"Ah, yes, here it is, Mr. Horton. It looks like your balance due comes to an even two thousand dollars, plus an additional four hundred dollars in interest for the year."

"That interest bill seems to be a little steep to me," responded Horton.

"Twenty percent per annum is the going rate here, Mister Horton. Take it or leave it."

"Suppose I can't make full payment. I expect that there would be no problem in extending the loan."

"You'd have to talk with Colonel Delacourte about that, Mister Horton, but it has been his policy not to renew loans. Times are hard, you know, and the bank needs its money."

"Well, since the loan was made in Confederate money, I suppose you have no objection to the payoff being made in the same tender."

Purdy blinked a couple of times and turned red around the collar. "Really, Mister Horton! The loan was made in the legal tender of the time and the bank demands payment in legal tender, preferably gold. You rebels should have thought twice before secession. Losing the war is no excuse for not paying your debts." Purdy felt he was back in control.

Horton reached into his shirt pocket and withdrew a piece of paper, which he passed to Purdy.

"This is a bank draft on a Washington bank. You will notice that it is in United States funds. I have properly endorsed it. Please be good enough to make the mortgage on the Circle H 'Paid.' I'd like the original note back, and I'll take the twenty-six-hundred-dollar difference between the bank draft and the mortgage in gold. Now."

"I ..., I ..." stammered Purdy. "I ... can't give you the gold until this draft clears the bank in Washington."

"Make out a receipt for the draft then, and wire Washington for verification. I want the receipt and the note now. I'll be back this afternoon for the gold. Have it ready. I charge twenty percent interest on loans, too."

Purdy complied with Horton's instructions and passed him the original note, marked "Paid," and a receipt for the bank draft.

"I'll be back at four. Have the gold ready then," Horton instructed. From his tone and bearing, Purdy had no question about Horton being serious.

Horton tucked the papers into his shirt pocket as he left the bank. He smiled to himself. It was clear to him that in these hard times, the bank, which was to say Delacourte, did not expect people to be able to repay loans. There was little doubt in his mind that Delacourte had taken over the bank as a means of acquiring local property cheaply. Finding notes for loans made during the war had been a bonus for him. Horton doubted that these notes for loans made in Confederate currency were legally collectable, but he felt that he had a moral obligation to make restitution. What bothered him was that Delacourte would get the money, not the men who had advanced the loan.

Horton had several hours to kill before he was expected at the bank to pick up the balance of his money. That money constituted most of his accumulated pay for the past four years, and he planned to use it to put the ranch back on its feet.

He shifted the Henry to his right hand and started up the street towards the sheriff's office. Ira Watkins had been sheriff for ten years before the war, and Horton knew him to be an honest and brave man. If anyone could tell him where to find some good hands, it would be Ira.

As Horton walked past the hotel, a bearded man wearing a checked shirt collided with him.

"Watch where you're goin'," the man growled. He put his right hand on Horton's chest and started to push.

Horton took one step backward and swung the Henry in an arc, catching the man squarely on the side of his head with the barrel. The man let out a sigh and sank to the boardwalk, unconscious. Horton stepped over the inert form and started on his way again.

"Just a minute, mister," a voice to his left demanded.

Horton stopped and raised the muzzle of his Henry until the barrel rested in the crook of his left arm. As he raised the muzzle, Horton turned his head towards the speaker, thumbing back the hammer on his rifle as he turned.

"Take it easy, mister. I just want to talk with you for a minute."

A man of medium height emerged from the hotel entrance. He wore a clean, black suit, a gray vest, and a wide-brimmed, low-crowned black hat. Horton could not see a gun, but a bulge under the man's left armpit suggested that the man might be carrying a pistol there.

"That was my man you just hit. When he wakes up, he'll probably come looking for you."

"I'm big enough to be easy to find. You can tell him I'll be up the street near the sheriff's office if he wants a rematch. I've got to tell you, though, if he's your man, you don't have much to brag on."

"Mister, I can use a man like you. Are you looking for a job?"

"I've got one at the Circle H," responded Horton, watching the expression of the other man.

"You might not have one for long, stranger. That ranch is about to fold. You'd do well to reconsider and work for me at the Rafter T. I'm Colonel Delacourte. I own the bank and most of the rest of this town."

"My name's Horton, and I'm betting that the Circle H stays in operation for quite a spell."

Delacourte's face registered a brief look of surprise. "So, you're Horton. I thought that all you boys got killed with Hood during the war."

"The war didn't get us all, and we weren't all with Hood," Horton responded.

"Let's go next door to my place," Delacourte said, indicating a saloon, "and I'll buy you a drink. I think we've got some business to discuss."

"What sort of business?" asked Horton.

Delacourte stepped closer to Horton and lowered his voice. "I'm not in the habit of discussing business in the middle of the street. We can be more comfortable at my place, and half the town won't be listening to what we have to say."

Horton hesitated. Instinctive dislike for Delacourte swelled within him. Horton also knew that if he was going to make the Circle H a paying ranch again, he was going to clash with Delacourte eventually. He decided that he had better take the opportunity to learn more of the man before the fight.

"Lead the way, Delacourte," Horton responded.

Delacourte turned and led the way to the saloon. As they entered the building, Horton saw that the saloon was rather plush by frontier standards. To his right, a mirrored bar ran the length of the room and a dozen wooden tables with chairs occupied the area to his left. The only light came from the windows along the front of the building and the single window next to a door at the rear. Several lamps were scattered around the room for nighttime use. The plank floor was swept clean, and there was sawdust around the cuspidors. Two men lounged at the far end of the bar.

Delacourte told the bartender to bring a bottle and two glasses. He walked to a table in the back corner of the room and sat down facing the room. Horton moved his chair close to Delacourte's right.

"I don't like sitting with my back to the room either."

Delacourte chuckled and moved his chair to give Horton more room. Horton laid the Henry on the table and turned to his left to look at Delacourte.

"Like I said, what business do we have to discuss?"

Delacourte waited until the bartender placed the bottle and two glasses on the table and departed. He poured two drinks and pushed one towards Horton.

"I'd like to buy the Circle H. I'm building a larger ranch around the old Rafter T. I can use the graze and the water on your place. How about it?

"Not interested," said Horton. He left his drink untouched on the table.

"You might be a bit premature," Delacourte responded. "Money is scarce around here, and you have a bank note due in two weeks. If you can't meet the note, then I'll get the Circle H anyway. If you sell now, at least you will have a grubstake to start somewhere else. Turn me down and you'll end up with nothin'."

Horton allowed a tight smile to crease his face. "Wrong, Delacourte. It's you that's premature. I paid that banknote off not twenty minutes ago. The Circle H is not for sale, in whole or in part, now or ever."

A look of surprise and then one of anger crossed Delacourte's face. "Just how did a Reb like you get that kind of money?" he snorted.

"Mostly, I got it from honest labor. I recommend it to you highly. How did you happen to come by yours, Delacourte?"

Delacourte reddened and pushed back his chair. "Just what are you implying, Horton?"

"Nothing more or less than you implied before," replied Horton as he pushed back his chair. He stood up slowly. "I don't think that we have anything more to discuss, Delacourte."

"It's 'Colonel Delacourte' to you and your kind," he snarled. Delacourte, too, got to his feet.

Horton looked Delacourte slowly up and down, as if measuring him, and said, "The only other man I ever knew who insisted on being called by a rank he longer wore was a cheap four-flusher who had never earned the rank in the first place. That makes me real suspicious of you."

Delacourte started to speak but Horton cut him off.

"You've said enough for today, Delacourte. You've had your own way around here for quite a while. You've bought a lot of property too cheap from folks having a hard time and you've pushed people out who wanted to stay. I'm giving you notice that I'm staying, and if I get pushed, I push back. Hard!"

Horton picked up his Henry and edged his way to the door. By that time, Delacourte had fought down his rage sufficiently to shout at Horton, "We're not finished yet, Reb!"

Horton ignored him. Glancing quickly behind him to make sure that the way was clear, Horton backed through the door, turned quickly and started back up the street towards the sheriff's office. He still wanted to see Sheriff Watkins.

As he walked along the boardwalk, Horton reviewed his encounter with Delacourte. Nothing had been settled in the saloon. He had learned that Delacourte angered easily and acted on incomplete knowledge. Delacourte had assumed that Horton had served with the Confederacy, assumed that the Circle H note was still due and that Horton could not pay it, and assumed that Horton would leave the territory rather than fight. Horton filed away these bits of information in his memory for future use. He walked briskly up the street, ignoring the dull pain in his right leg. It felt good to be back in action again, even if it was only against somebody such as Delacourte.

Delacourte was in a rage. "Who does that Horton think he is? Jock, what in hell were you and Whitey doing just standing there? Why did you let him get out of here?"

"Boss, we didn't know you wanted him to stay," replied Jock, who was a short, stocky man with a week's growth of beard on his face. "Besides, he had the hammer back on that Henry an' he looked like he'd enjoy usin' it."

"Fools!" Delacourte ranted. "I'm surrounded by fools. Do I have to do everything myself? If you can find your way to the door, go get Brannon. Now!"

Jock and Whitey fled through the doorway, getting tangled up and nearly falling in the process. Delacourte could only shake his head. Four minutes later, they came back with Brannon. By that time, Delacourte was back in control of himself.

Max Brannon was forty-years old and looked as though each of those years had been a hard one. His two hundred pounds were distributed evenly over his six-foot frame, although the start of a paunch was just visible below his gun belt. He had spent the war enlisting in Union regiments to collect the bounty and then deserting as soon as it was paid. When the money was gone, he enlisted somewhere else, under a new name. He had killed several men while in Delacourte's employ. He favored back shooting, not because he was afraid to face his opponents, but because this method usually produced a sure kill. He liked working for Delacourte because the pay was good and the work was easy.

Brannon joined Delacourte at the table in the rear of the room and sat down in the chair that Horton had vacated a few minutes before. Delacourte got right to the point.

"Brannon, a Horton just left here. I want you to find out which one he is and what he's up to. I want one of the boys to keep an eye on him."

"Colonel, I had Charlie out to the Horton place yesterday. He seen some rider come in around mid-morin' an' leave around dusk. From the description he gave, and the one Jock just gave me of Horton, I'd say they was the same man."

"Well, he didn't leave," replied Delacourte. "Get that information I want and then get right back here. Horton's got to go. We can't have one man upsetting our plans. Whatever we've achieved has been because our opponents have not worked together. This man Horton looks like he could be the leader that the rest of these people around here have been looking for."

As he stood up, Brannon replied, "I'll get started right away, Colonel. He can't be too tough."

"Don't underestimate him. He could be real trouble," Delacourte warned. Brannon just smiled thinly and walked out.

Horton found the sheriff's office just as he remembered it. Ira Watkins had changed little, although perhaps he was a little grayer and a little thinner. His piercing gray eyes gave a twinkle of recognition as Horton walked into the room.

"Damn me, if it ain't Seth Horton. How're you doin', boy? We all thought you was dead."

"Ira, I've talked with four people since I've been back, and three of them have told me that I was dead.

The fourth man never heard of me, so he really doesn't count. I'm a little worried that you all might know something I don't. I may just hit the next person who tells me that I'm dead."

Ira laughed. "It's good to have you back here. A lot of the boys haven't come home, and probably never will. The whole war was a damned foolish adventure for most folks around here. We was never a big slave state, an' all them states' rights issues was kinda cloudy by the time they drifted out here. The war was big fun until the casualty reports started comin' back instead of the boys. Families lost their sons, then their money and property, and then their self-respect. I don't think that there's a family in the county that ain't been hurt by this foolishness."

"Well, it's over now," responded Horton. "You seem to have fared pretty well. How's Sarah?"

"Sarah's doin' well. She got married to that Jamison boy by Austin in '62. He died sometime in '63 of a fever. The grave's someplace in Virginia. He 'n' Sarah had less than a week together before he went off. That's probably part of the reason why I'm bitter about the war an' all."

The men sat in silence for a few moments, each lost in his own thoughts. Finally, Horton spoke.

"I just left a man named Delacourte. He tried to buy the Circle H and when I wouldn't sell, he made some threats. What do you know about him?"

Ira filled Horton in on what little he knew of Delacourte, verifying what Joe had told him. He learned little else, except that Delacourte had claimed to have been a member of Phil Sheridan's staff. "Very interesting," thought Horton. "I wonder what rock he was hiding under to keep me from ever seeing him?"

Just then the office door opened and Sarah walked into the room. "Dad," she said, "I thought you were coming home for lunch. Where have ... Seth! I thought that you were dead!"

Ira and Seth looked at each other and laughed. Sarah looked perplexed. After a moment or two, Ira explained.

"Seth said that everyone he's met has said that they thought he was dead and he was goin' to hit the next one who said it. 'Peers to me that you're about to get hit."

Sarah threw up her hands in mock terror. "Please sir, don't hurt me. I didn't mean it. Really, I didn't!"

They all laughed. Sarah walked over and hugged Seth. "It's good to have you home. Are you going to stay?"

Horton smiled and said, "I don't really know, Sarah. Right now, Delacourte wants to take over the Circle H any way he can. If he tries, he'll find himself in one hell of a fight. I'm hoping that my brothers will turn up so we can decide what to do with the ranch. Until they do, I plan on running the place."

For the next few minutes, they all talked about old times and people they knew. When they were finished, Horton was well on his way to being caught up on the local news.

"Ira," Horton said, "I've got to find a few hands. Do you know of anyone who would be suitable? I don't want any gunmen like Delacourte's hired, but they'd have to know that a little danger might go with the job."

"I can think of four or five that might be suitable, but the fact is that I don't know if they'd be willin' to work for you."

Seth looked puzzled. "Why?" he asked.

"These boys all wore gray, Seth, and that blue coat you wore ain't any too popular around here. They may look on any fight between you and Delacourte as one Yankee bein' done in by another and no matter what happens, they're winners. Sorry to be so blunt about it, boy, but feelin's about Yankees run deep around here, an' a lot of folks still look on you as a traitor."

Horton was surprised. It had never occurred to him that he would be seen as a villain. He had gone north because he could not break the oath he took when he was commissioned on the plain at West Point, even though many others had. He had done his duty as he had seen it, no more and no less. For this he was being called a traitor?

He turned to the sheriff and cleared his throat. "Thanks, Ira. I see what you mean. I'd appreciate it if you'd try, anyway. As far as I'm concerned, the war's over. I hope some others besides us think the same way. I could use some hands, but I can get by without them."

After a few minutes, Horton collected his Henry and went back to the bank for his horse. He rode the bay to the livery, where he fed and watered him. Then, he went up into the loft and stretched out on the hay. He still had more than three hours to wait before he could pick up his money. As he lay there, he pondered over what to do about the ranch, but there were far too many questions left for him to reach any conclusions. He also thought of Sarah, twenty-five now, a lovely widow and one of the few people he could truthfully call a friend. He thought of Delacourte, too, and of the inevitable struggle between them. He drifted off into a fitful slumber.

At four o'clock, Horton entered the bank, rifle in his right hand and saddle bags over his shoulder. Mister Purdy was very nervous. He tugged at his collar and said, "Colonel Delacourte was most upset. It will not be possible for you to withdraw the whole amount today. We don't keep that much gold on hand. Robbers, you know."

Horton looked at Purdy until Purdy looked away. Horton spoke quietly, but with force. "Purdy, if I don't get that money, and right now, I'll start the biggest run this bank has ever seen." He rested the muzzle of the Henry on the counter. "You won't see it, though. You'll be dead. I suggest that you don't test me to see if I'm bluffing. I assure you that I am serious." Horton tossed the saddle bags to Purdy with his left hand. "Fill 'em," he said.

Purdy was so frightened that he was afraid he would soil himself. He knew that this crazy Texan was absolutely serious. He filled the saddle bags with twenty-six hundred dollars' worth of double eagles and handed the bags back to Horton. To hell with Delacourte, Purdy thought, he's not looking down the barrel of that cannon. I can always find myself another town and another bank if I have to.

Horton flipped the receipt for the bank draft onto the counter and, hefting the saddle bags, left the bank. As he rode out of town, he thought he saw a man wearing a checked shirt and a bandage on his head following him, but he couldn't be sure. Nevertheless, Horton rode home cautiously.

He knew that he had won the first round, but the fight would be a long one. Delacourte could afford to lose a round; he could not. He was relieved when the ranch headquarters came into view and Joe came out to meet him.

The man with the checked shirt was called Ox by the rest of Delacourte's crew. As he moved into position overlooking the ranch house, he cursed Max Brannon for sending him out to keep Horton in sight. He longed to see Horton in the sights of the rifle he carried, but some instinct warned him that his first shot had better be a good one or there would never be a chance for a second. Still cursing, Ox settled in for a long, cold night.

Chapter 5

Horton walked out into the crisp spring air. The sun was just climbing over the horizon, turning the light sprinkling of frost into a kaleidoscope of color. He finished buttoning his coat, pulled on his gloves and headed for the barns to check the stock. He had just finished a huge breakfast of beefsteak, eggs, and coffee, and was at peace with the world.

It had been three months since he had ridden into Benton to pay off the note on the ranch. During those months, significant change had taken place at the Circle H. Perhaps the most important change had been the hiring of Pepe Mendoza, a gnarled old man of indeterminable age who had proven himself to be the best cook in the state of Texas. Pepe had been the first of five hands that Horton had hired. True to his word, Ira Watkins had sent Pepe and two other men to Horton and two more men had drifted in looking for work. Horton was well satisfied with his crew and all that they had accomplished. Long-delayed repairs to the main ranch headquarters buildings had been completed, the north line shack rebuilt, and a large stock corral had been started.

A noticeable change had taken place in Seth, too. The hard work had stressed him, but that stress had added more than twenty pounds of muscle to his frame. His hospital pallor had entirely disappeared, having been replaced by the healthy, weathered appearance of one who performs hard physical labor outdoors. Although his right leg still pained him from time to time, he had lost all trace of a limp. Seth felt rejuvenated.

Not all the change in Seth was the result of hard work. From the first, he had been making weekly visits to Benton, supposedly to check on inquiries he had made into the whereabouts of his brothers, but always ending with a visit to Sarah. More recently those trips had increased in frequency to the point where Ira Watkins had begun to hint that he thought it was time for Sarah to start looking for another husband.

Somewhat to his dismay, Seth found himself seriously considering the prospect of marriage. He had always been too busy for a family before, and the uncertainty of Army life on the frontier and during the war had made serious courting nearly impossible. Now there seemed to be time for such things and he could no more deny the feelings that he held for Sarah than she could those she felt for him. The excitement and barely restrained promise of passion each felt for the other was clearly visible whenever they were together. Seth smiled to himself. Things were definitely getting serious, and he was enjoying every minute of it.

The only flaw in this seemingly ideal situation was the continuing tension between Horton and Delacourte. Although there had been no further clashes between the two or any of their riders, Horton continued to find fresh signs that the ranch headquarters was being kept under continued observation. He and Joe Penbrook had taken to making patrols around the place at odd hours, more to keep the observers off balance than to end the observations. Twice they had managed to sneak close enough to run off the watcher's horse, giving the observer the opportunity for making the long trip back to town on foot. High-heeled boots guaranteed that such a trip would be quite painful, at least towards the end.

Mister Purdy had vanished suddenly. This disappearance was the topic of considerable speculation among the townsfolk. The most popular theory was that Delacourte had either done Purdy in for giving gold to Horton or had run him off for the same reason. This theory was closely rivaled by one which contended that Horton had performed the running-off or doing-in because Purdy had tried to forestall payment. The truth of the matter was that Mister Purdy had stuffed a valise with greenbacks and had taken a roundabout route to Albany, New York, where he had set himself up in the hotel business. He preferred customers who did not carry Henrys.

Delacourte had been furious when he discovered the money was gone, but he would rather have cut out his own tongue than to admit that Purdy had bested him. He had sent Max Brannon and a dozen men to find Purdy, but they had lost the trail in Austin. Delacourte was certain that Purdy was in Mexico, living it up, but he was praying fervently that Purdy was rotting in hell.

Seth met Joe at the main barn. "Boss, I just sent the boys out to start drivin' whatever stock they find down to the valley floor. I believe we oughta get a count of what we got so we can see if we should sell off an' start over or what."

Seth thought for a minute. "Good plan, Joe. I don't have any idea what the rustlers left for us. There isn't much of a market for cows around here and I'd eat them myself before I'd sell them to Delacourte. If it comes to a sale, we might have to move a herd to a railhead and ship those steers to market. It might be worthwhile talking to the ranchers east of here to see what they've got in the way of steers to sell or ship. Maybe we can put together a herd big enough to bring in some real money."

"Believe I had better handle that. Maybe you should go to town an' see about findin' us a market." Joe's eyes danced mischievously. He knew very well that Seth would not pass up any legitimate reason for going into town.

"I think you and Ira Watkins are plotting against me, old man. Still, it wouldn't hurt to see if there's a market for Texas beef somewhere. I believe I might just take that little trip to town."

"Thought you might, seein' how you shaved an' put lilac water on, an' all. Your horse's all saddled an' ready."

"Sometimes you take too much for granted, Penbrook," Seth said gruffly, but his dancing eyes and faint smile suggested that perhaps this was not one of those times.

Horton collected his horse and rode back to the house to get his Henry. Joe met him on the porch with the rifle and Horton's pistol belt.

"Maybe I'm getting to be too predictable," said Horton.

"Maybe so. Maybe you're gettin' a might careless, too. Take the big Colt along with you. That little hideout you tote don't make you look like you're serious."

"The rifle's enough," responded Horton, but he took the gun belt anyway and slid it into the saddle bag. He slid the Henry into its scabbard and wheeled his horse.

"I'll see you sometime tomorrow," Horton said as he started towards town. Joe just tossed him what barely passed for a salute and smiled.

"Maybe I'll see him tomorrow, maybe I won't. In the springtime, it ain't natural for a young man's attention to be on cows," Joe philosophized to himself as he watched Horton disappear among the trees.

As he rode to town, Horton thought about the other ranchers around him, evaluating each for the potential to contribute to a herd. The number of possible participants had grown smaller during the last three months. Two had packed up and left, leaving Delacourte to take over their range. Max Brannon had shot another in a gunfight. Still others were worried about losing their property to back taxes or overdue notes to the bank and would do nothing that might anger Delacourte.

Horton could only think of three or four ranchers who might be willing to take a chance on a trail drive scheme, especially if Horton were involved. Ira Watkins had been accurate in his statement that Horton's blue uniform had not endeared him to the locals. The town and surrounding ranchers were taking a "wait and see" attitude towards the Horton-Delacourte feud. The ranchers would have a harder time turning down any proposal if Joe Penbrook made it instead of Horton, and they both knew it.

As was his custom, Horton exercised caution during his ride to town. He seldom followed the same exact route twice, hoping in that way to make it more difficult to spring an ambush. Of course, at some point he had to strike the main road unless he wanted to swing wide around the town and enter from a different direction, but he was reluctant to do that. He did not want Delacourte to know that he was causing him any problems. He did ride carefully, however, and his eyes were never still. His horse, the same big bay Joe and caught for him when he first arrived at the Circle H, seemed to sense his rider's caution. The horse had become alert as his rider, and for the hundredth time, Horton was thankful to have such an animal.

Horton thought about Delacourte as he rode, and not for the first time wondered who he really was. Horton had known all the field grade and most of the company grade officers who had served on Sheridan's staff. Delacourte had not been among them. Horton wondered why Delacourte maintained the charade and what purpose such a misrepresentation served. Horton had written his old friend Captain (Brevet Colonel) Donovan with a description of Delacourte, hoping that he might remember him. He had also written to the military commander at New Orleans for the same information. So far, he had heard from neither. Horton knew that both letters were longshots. The probability that either man had known Delacourte was slight.

Horton rode into town and stopped in front of the only general store still not controlled by Delacourte. Since he always paid in cash, his business was welcome there. The owner, Tad Beckley, had finally begun to greet him with civility. Beckley's two sons had been killed while serving with the Confederate Army, and Horton could understand the man's cool attitude. Horton placed his order for the supplies he needed and made arrangements for their delivery to the ranch. He dropped his horse off at the livery and walked up the street to the sheriff's office.

Ira Watkins had continued to make inquiries for him as to the whereabouts of his brothers, but Horton was beginning to doubt that they would produce much. That they were still alive he had little doubt. All the boys, himself included, had been encouraged to display independence for as long as he could remember. The result had been five tough men who thought quickly and clearly, and who could be counted upon in a crisis. He knew that one of his brothers had been killed, but Horton firmly believed that the other three would eventually return home. He only wished that it would be soon.

The sheriff's office proved to be empty and a check at his house produced the same result. Horton knocked on a neighbor's door and learned from the somewhat belligerent lady of the house that Sheriff Watkins and his daughter had left that morning for Austin, purpose unknown, thank you. Horton thanked the lady for her trouble and apologized for inconveniencing her. Swallowing his disappointment in having missed Sarah, he headed back to the livery stable. To make a bad day worse, the storm clouds that had been gathering as he rode into town picked that moment to rupture and disgorge enough water to strangle a frog. Horton hurried into a doorway that proved to belong to Jenkins' saloon. Horton went inside and dusted the water from his jacket with his hat.

Horton let his eyes sweep the room. It was a standard saloon for the day, with a bar made of planks set across upended barrels located to the right of the door and five or six tables with chairs scattered around the remainder of the room. The plank floor was layered with sawdust and the dirty windows along the front filtered the little light that penetrated the darkening clouds outside. A bartender was polishing a glass with little enthusiasm, and four drifters were playing cards in the corner. A door in the back led to an alley. No one even looked up when Horton entered.

Horton stepped up to the bar and ordered a beer. The bartender seemed to resent the interruption but slid a beer in front of him anyway. Horton turned around, hooked his elbows over the bar, and surveyed the room again. The men at the table finished playing the hand and looked up. Spotting Horton at the bar, a bearded youth wearing a confederate cape invited him to join the game. Horton declined politely and bought them a round of beer. He continued to watch as the game resumed.

Across the street, Max Brannon saw Horton enter the saloon. He turned to Jock and said, "Take Charlie and Ox across the street to the saloon. Horton just went in there. Make sure he stays there while I get the colonel."

Jock looked at him as if Max had suddenly lost his mind. "You're sure you wanna do that? If there's any trouble, Watkins'll throw us all in the jug." Ox rubbed the left side of his head and smiled wickedly.

"Watkins is out of town," said Max. "You go take care of Horton while I get the boss. He may want to settle this thing today."

Jock, Charlie, and Ox adjusted their hats and stepped out into the rain. They moved quickly across the street and entered the saloon, stomping mud and water from their boots.

"Well, looky who's here," Ox bellowed. "If'n it ain't the big man with the Henry. Where's your Henry now, big man?"

Horton cursed silently under his breath. Maybe Joe's right, he thought, maybe I am getting careless. His Henry was in its scabbard at the livery, along with his saddle bags containing the big Colt.

Ox moved to the far end of the bar to Horton's right while Jock and Charlie moved up on his left. The four men playing cards put down their hands and rose slowly. Making no sudden moves, they drifted through the door into the alley. The bartender moved down to the end of the bar near Ox and made it perfectly clear that he was not going to take part in any fight. Ox looked somewhat disappointed.

Jock turned his attention back to Horton. "Heard that you was gatherin' cows out of the brush. Heard you ain't too damn particular whose brand's on 'em, either. What do you have to say about that, big man?"

Horton sighed. There was no way he was going to be able to avoid a fight. He was a little surprised to find that he really didn't want to. He felt sudden excitement flow through his veins.

"You're not very careful about your facts, Jock." Horton looked at Ox and Charlie, then continued. "You don't appear to be very careful about who you hang around with, either."

"You callin' me a liar?" Jock asked angrily.

"Take it whatever way you want."

Jock took four steps away from the bar, reached down and pulled a knife from his boot. "Alright, big man, I'm goin' to trim you down to size. In fact, when I get done, I'm gonna gut you like a fish."

"I hope you've brought your lunch, Jock, because it might take you quite a while to get the job done."

Jock started to move towards Horton while Ox moved out into the room, away from the bar. Charlie stayed where he was, leaning on the bar.

Jock crouched, knife held low. Horton moved forward, his weight balanced on the balls of his feet. Jock tried a couple of tentative slashes, which Horton easily avoided. With the next slash, Horton stepped forward and grabbed Jock's right wrist with his left hand. At the same time, he kneed Jock violently in the groin. As Jock's breath exploded through his open mouth, Horton quickly stepped up beside Jock and smashed his right forearm into Jock's face as he kicked backward with his right foot, knocking Jock's right leg out from under him. Jock landed with a crash on the rough plank floor. Still holding onto Jock's right wrist, Horton delivered a tremendous kick to his right armpit. He was rewarded with the sound of ripping muscle and breaking bone. Jock passed out without making a sound.

From the corner of his eye, Horton saw Ox draw his pistol. Horton reached for the Colt at the small of his back as he turned toward Ox. He saw white smoke mushroom from the barrel of Ox's Colt and felt a tremendous blow strike his right hip. Not that leg again, he thought as he completed his draw and fired at Ox's chest. As he fell, Horton saw Ox's right eye disappear and the back of his head erupt with blood, bone, and brain tissue a split second later. Ox was dead before he even began to fall. The thought that he had nearly missed Ox altogether flashed across Horton's mind, followed immediately by relief at having hit him hard enough to take him out of the fight permanently.

Horton struck the floor and rolled to his right, lining the sights of his pistol on Charlie's belly as he cocked the weapon. Charlie had nearly completed drawing his Colt.

"Do you have any great desire to buy into this fight, Charlie?" Horton asked.

"No sir, I sure don't."

"Have you any place to go, like maybe Mexico or Canada?"

"Yes, sir! I believe I could go right away, too."

"Then go, Charlie. But if I ever see you again, you're a dead man. Do you understand me?"

Charlie nodded nervously, dropped his pistol back into its holster, and turned towards the door. This is my chance, Charlie thought. As he walked through the doorway, he dropped his hand to the butt of his pistol, turned, and drew.

Horton saw Charlie hesitate at the doorway and fired just as Charlie's gun cleared the holster. The slug caught him just above the belt buckle. Charlie staggered backwards but continued to raise his pistol. Horton's second shot caught him in the chest and drove him through the doorway and out onto the boardwalk. Charlie collapsed, rolled onto his belly, and died.

Horton turned towards the bartender, who had both hands flat on the planks of the bar and was swallowing nervously. "I ... I got no part in this f-fight," he stammered.

Using a chair for support, Horton pulled himself to his feet. Shifting the pistol to his left hand, he ran his right over his hip. He found that Ox's bullet had hit him just behind the right hip bone, perhaps nicking it. The exit wound was near the center of the buttock. Horton removed his knife from his pocket and cut two pieces of cloth from his bandana. These he used to plug both ends of the wound. He staggered to the bar and reached behind it to get a bottle of whiskey.

"I'll pay for this later," he said, and stumbled through the front doorway.

Horton knew that he had only seconds to get away. If someone hadn't alerted Delacourte and the rest of his crew, the four shots would have. With Sheriff Watkins gone, Horton had absolutely no hope of anyone in authority stepping forward to prevent more violence. He was on his own, and he knew it. He also knew that he was in no shape to stay and fight.

Another wave of pain hit him as he moved to the hitching rack. As he moved past Charlie's body, Horton saw the 1851 Navy Colt that Charlie had dropped. It contained five loads, while his own only had one left. Horton knew that he might need the firepower and Charlie wouldn't, so he replaced his own pistol and scooped up Charlie's.

Horton untied the first horse he came to, pulled himself into the saddle, and rode to the livery. He rode straight through the doorway and swung from the saddle, almost passing out from the pain when his feet hit the ground. The hostler shrank away from him, but Horton ordered him to saddle his bay. As soon as the horse was ready, Horton swung into the saddle, grinding his teeth from the pain the movement caused. He knew that he was hard hit, although he was not bleeding as badly as before. The last numbness from the initial shock of the slug had worn off completely and he nearly cried out as he settled into the saddle.

Horton gathered up the reins with his left hand and, still holding Charlie's Colt in his right, rode swiftly from the livery and out of town. As he passed the burned-out church, he heard two shots from behind him, but he could not hear the passing of the slugs. Shooting wild, he thought, as the horse thundered through the mud towards the ranch.

About a mile outside of town, Horton pulled up under a large cottonwood tree. He secured the Colt and stuffed more of the bandana into the wound. The pain blurred his sight and he felt lightheaded. Horton urged the horse back onto the trail. He knew that he would never make it back to the ranch on his own. He tied his hands to the saddle horn and turned the horse's head loose. Shortly after that, Horton passed out.

When he came to, Horton had absolutely no idea of where he was. He saw that he was in a draw, and he knew that the rain had let up to a slow drizzle. From the lengthening shadows, he calculated that he had been unconscious for several hours. Confused and disoriented, Horton freed himself from the saddle horn and urged the horse deeper into the draw until he came upon a small spring or a large puddle. It was difficult to tell the difference because of the rain and the poor light.

Horton eased himself to the ground, removed the bridle from the horse, and uncinched the saddle. The horse shied and the saddle fell to the ground. Horton dragged himself to the shelter of a windfall and rolled up in his saddle blanket. He passed out again almost immediately. He never heard the horse as it ran off towards the ranch.

Chapter 6

Delacourte heard the shots in the saloon just as Max Brannon found him. Brannon explained quickly what he had done.

"Maybe Jock and the boys killed the bastard," Delacourte said hopefully as he put on his coat. He picked up a shotgun and headed for the street.

Delacourte reached the street just in time to see Horton ride out from the livery. Although he knew that he was well out of range, Delacourte raised the shotgun and fired both barrels after the fleeing Horton.

"Get the boys," Delacourte shouted to Brannon. He dropped the shotgun and ran down the street to the saloon, where he stepped over Charlie's body and found Ox dead inside. Jock was still unconscious.

Delacourte saw a pool of blood near the bar. He walked over to the bartender and asked, "Did you see what happened here?"

"I did, Colonel. That man there," he said as he pointed to the unconscious Jock, "came in here with the dead one and another man and pulled a knife on this guy Horton. Horton thumped that one and then that one," the bartender gestured, indicating Ox, "shot

Horton. Horton pulled a gun and killed him, then he killed the third man."

"All of this happened pretty fast, didn't it?"

"Yes sir, it surely did."

"It's possible that in all the confusion you got some of the facts mixed up, isn't it?"

"I saw it pretty clear, Colonel Delacourte."

"I'll tell you how it happened. Horton came in here and started a fight with my boys. He killed Ox and Charlie there and then ran for his life." Delacourte drew a pistol from beneath his coat and laid it menacingly on the bar. "That's what really happened, isn't it?"

"I ... I guess you're right, Colonel. In fact, I'm sure of it. It happened just like you said."

"If you know what's good for you, you won't change that story when the sheriff talks to you. You aren't going to disappoint me, are you?"

"No, sir. That's my story and I'll stick to it."

Delacourte put his pistol away and walked outside just as Brannon rode up with Delacourte's horse and half a dozen other riders.

"Max," Delacourte said, "You sent three fools to do a man's job. Ox did manage to get a slug into Horton, and from all the blood on the floor, I'd say that he was hit pretty hard. Ox and Charlie are dead, and Jock looks like he's fit to do nothing more than sweep floors. Since the law is out of town, we're going out to the Horton place and finish this fight now. Make sure somebody brings a rope."

Delacourte swung into the saddle and led his crowd out of town. It was still raining hard and after a few minutes all of the riders were soaking wet. Horton's tracks were completely obliterated and Delacourte gave up any thought of tracking him down. Instead, he rode directly for the Circle H, gambling that Horton would go there to seek aid.

Wet clothes and soft living produced a cold and miserable crew by the second hour of the ride. By the time Delacourte paused on the ridgeline overlooking the Circle H headquarters, it was clear that a halt must be called so that the final attack on the ranch could be organized.

Max Brannon dismounted his men on the far side of the ridge, out of sight of the ranch house. While Delacourte studied the ranch headquarters from the crest of the ridge, Brannon found some dry wood close in under the cedars and started a small fire. The rain had fallen off to little more than a mist and the fire helped raise the morale of the crew more than it actually warmed or dried them. Brannon made them check the loads in their weapons while he joined Delacourte on the ridge.

"What do you see, Colonel?"

"Not a thing, Brannon. There's smoke coming from the main house, but I can't see any movement at all. There's no smoke coming from the bunkhouse, and I can't see any stock in the stone corral."

"You think maybe Horton didn't come back here?"

"He had nowhere else to go. If he's not here, then he's back there somewhere along the way, most likely dead. He was hit too hard to do more than come here or die."

"I'm not too sure about that, Colonel. Horton's a damned tough man. If he ain't down there, we may be in for big trouble," Brannon warned.

"Damn it, Brannon, he's only one man!" Delacourte exploded. "If he's not down there, then he's out in the mesquite somewhere, dead. Even if he isn't dead now, he will be the first time he shows his face again. We can make a murder charge stick for the shootout at Jenkins' place."

"If you say so, Colonel. All I know is that I ain't goin' to mark him 'done' 'til I shovel dirt on his face."

The truth, thought Delacourte, is that I won't be able to either. Aloud, he said, "We'll go down the ridge together. Send two of the boys to check out the bunkhouse and the other buildings. Send two more around to the back of the house to make sure nobody gets out that easy. You and I will take the other two men with us and rush the front of the house. We'll start in ten minutes."

Brannon went back to organize the raid according to Delacourte's instructions. Delacourte stayed on the ridge until Brannon rode up with the rest of the men. Mounting his horse, Delacourte drew a Spencer carbine from its scabbard and led his men down off the ridge to the Circle H headquarters.

As they approached the ranch house, the four men designated by Brannon broke off to begin their search of the barns and other outbuildings. The remainder halted with Delacourte in front of the house.

"Hello, the house," Brannon hollered as he started to dismount.

The door opened and Pepe stepped out onto the porch. The Spencer he held in his hands steadied on Brannon's chest as he cocked the hammer.

"Do not bother to dismount, senor. The boss is not here, and I do not have time to talk."

Reluctantly, Brannon swung back into the saddle.

"You'll put that gun down if you know what's good for you, old man," said Delacourte. "We're looking for Horton and we're not leaving until we find him."

"Then you wait in the saddle, senor," Pepe said as he swung the muzzle of the Spencer to cover Delacourte.

As the muzzle shifted from Brannon to Delacourte, Brannon palmed his Colt and shot Pepe through the chest. As he fell, Pepe fired. The slug went wild, but the thunderous blast from Pepe's Spencer spooked Delacourte's horse.

Delacourte fought to control the terrified animal, but everything he did just made the situation worse. Finally, the horse succeeded in throwing Delacourte into the mud and ran off. Brannon sent one of the men to catch the horse.

Slowly, Delacourte got to his feet and attempted to brush the mud and water from his clothes. He soon gave up the attempt and focused his attention on Brannon.

"Damn you to hell, Brannon. What did you do that for? That old man could have killed me!"

"He didn't, though. You ain't never gonna get this place searched by settin' on a horse with your hands in the air. What was you fixin' to do, talk that old man to death?"

"Don't get smart with me, Brannon. Get the rest of the boys and search that damned house. But do it quickly. We've wasted enough time here as it is."

Brannon nodded and motioned to the two men who had checked the bunkhouse and barns to join him. The other man who had not gone after Delacourte's horse dismounted and joined the group. As Brannon neared the doorway, Pepe groaned. Brannon fired twice more into Pepe's body, finishing the murderous job he had started.

The search did not take long. It was plain that Pepe was the only man present at the Circle H. Delacourte was in a foul mood. He had counted on finding Horton either dead along the route or holed up here at the ranch. He had little liking for loose ends, and when that loose end was Horton, the potential for trouble was tremendous.

Delacourte turned to Brannon and said, "Set fire to anything that will burn. I don't want anything left that Horton can use. Put that old man's body on a horse. We'll take him off a ways and bury him."

"We can just put it in one of the lofts when we burn the barns. There won't be nothin' left to find."

"I said we'd bury him away from here. Now put his body on a horse and get those fires started." Delacourte stomped off towards Jake, who had caught Delacourte's horse and was riding up to the house with him.

"Someday, we're going to tangle, Delacourte," Brannon muttered under his breath. "Then we'll see who gives the orders around here." Aloud, he shouted, "Don't just stand there. You heard the Colonel. Set fire to anything that will burn."

The men scattered to follow their orders. Soon smoke was pouring from the barns, bunkhouse, and the outbuildings. Brannon and two of his men smashed the sparse furnishings in the house and broke oil lamps over the wreckage before firing the main house. Flames licked hungrily at the wreckage and Brannon and his men left the building.

Out in the yard, Brannon discovered that someone had caught up an extra horse for Pepe's body. Delacourte rode up to the group.

"Brannon, tomorrow I want you to move cattle onto this range. I don't want any riders around these buildings but post a lookout on the ridge in case Horton or that foreman of his shows up. After you get the cattle moved, I want a thorough search made of the area between the town and this ranch. I want Horton's body found and buried. Now let's get out of here."

Brannon nodded and wheeled his horse away from the burning house. The horses, smelling the smoke and feeling the heat from the flames, were becoming nervous and difficult to hold. As they rode away from the ranch, Delacourte shouted to Brannon.

"Have Jake bury that body a mile or so south of here. Make sure he plants him deep. I don't want that body found."

Brannon waved in acknowledgment and started to drop back to break the news to Jake. A fine reward for catchin' the old man's horse, he thought, but could be worse, I guess—he could send Jake back to the ridge to watch the ranch."

"And tell Jake when he's done with the old man to go back up to the ridge and keep an eye on the ranch."

Brannon waved again and rode back to Jake before Delacourte could think of something else.

It was nearly dark when the first of the Circle H riders, Pete Calhoun, showed up at the ranch headquarters. He was greeted by the smoking ruins of the barns and outbuildings. Only the stone walls of the barns remained standing. The house had not burned well.

Gun in hand, the rider probed the depths of the building. The wrecked furniture had burned briskly, but the high ceilings and adobe and stone walls were only blackened by smoke. Most of the roof over the lowerceilinged kitchen had burned, but aside from that, the house was intact.

He saw the pool of dried blood on the porch and called out to Pepe. His voice echoed through the deserted house. When he received no answer, the rider went back to his horse in the yard.

Within the hour, the remaining three riders had ridden into the yard. Each of the riders walked silently through the ruins to see for himself what had been done.

Pete spoke first. "Well, what are we gonna do?"

Shorty Burquest, one of the men who Sheriff Watkins had sent to the ranch, said, "Somebody ought to go to the town and tell the sheriff. Me, I'm gettin' the hell out of here. I didn't hire on to be no damned hired gun in somebody else's fight."

There was a murmur of agreement from the rest.

Luke Brown spoke up. "That goes for me, too. I'd like to know whose blood that is on the porch, though."

The last of the men, known only as Panhandle, said, "You can mess around tryin' to find out if you want, but I'm lightin' a shuck outta here before whoever got that blood aflowin' in the first place comes back. I ain't goin' into town, neither. If you feel strong about tellin' the sheriff, Shorty, then you go do it. I'm leavin'."

Shorty looked at the ground and moved some mud around with the toe of his right boot. "I don't feel any too good about ridin' off and leavin' the boss to handle this thing all by hisself. He done good by us an' helped us out when we needed it. We owe him something for that."

"We got wages comin', too," Pete reminded them.

"To hell with the wages, and to hell with Horton. That's probably his blood on the porch. We ain't any gun hands, an' I got a feelin' that any payoff here's gonna be in lead," Panhandle responded. "We never owed him nuthin' anyhow."

The group nodded in agreement. Now that their decision was made, they swiftly mounted their horses and rode off to the east. The rain continued to hiss as it cooled the ashes of the fire, and the last of the coals were stone cold long before the sun rose the next morning.

Chapter 7

Horton woke up to a world filled with pain. It was a red hot, throbbing thing that at first drove him from a comfortable blackness and then blocked out everything else from his consciousness. Slowly he became aware of other things. The smell of mud, the wet horse blanket over him, the rock poking into his side, and the pool of water in which he lay—all of these came crowding into his consciousness. But the center of it all, the hub of his existence, was still the pain.

He ground his teeth as he sat up. The horizon tipped alarmingly for a few moments, then settled back into its normal position. Horton leaned back against the fallen tree that had been providing him a degree of protection from the rain and waited for his vision to clear. The rain was still falling gently and felt good against his feverish face. He was soaked to the skin from the rain and the water in which he had been lying. He shivered violently.

Horton knew that he would never make it to his feet. His hip was a sea of flame that threatened at any moment to consume him. He started to crawl toward his saddle a dozen feet away. It took him many minutes to make the trip. Horton fumbled with the buckles on the saddle bags and finally got them opened. He pulled out his Colt and pistol belt and set them on the ground close at hand. He found that the bottle of whiskey he had taken from the saloon was miraculously unbroken after the fall from the horse. "The saddle must have cushioned the shock," he muttered to himself.

Horton knew that he must clean or cauterize the wound before fever, blood poisoning, or gangrene succeeded where Ox had failed. He was also sure that once the task of cleaning the wound was completed, it was unlikely that he would be able to do much for himself for some time. Slowly he set about establishing a campsite.

He untied the bedroll and the saddle bags from behind the saddle and dragged them back to the windfall. He found a relatively dry spot and used the groundsheet to form an overhead cover. The yellow slicker he always carried became an acceptable ground cover. Horton crawled back to the saddle and removed the canteen and the Henry. He retrieved the pistol and belt from the ground and moved back to the shelter he had made.

Horton needed many things, but what he felt most urgently was the need to be warm. He stripped off his sodden coat and shirt and put on the dry shirt from the spare change of clothes that he, like most riders, carried in his bedroll just for such emergencies. He could not remove his boots or his trousers. Horton spread out his blankets and placed the pistol from his bedroll with his other pistol and the belt next to the Henry, all within easy reach. He removed the pistol from the small of his back and put it, along with the pistol he had taken from Charlie, in one pocket of the saddle bag. Since they had been laying with him in a puddle of water for several hours, it was probable that the loads were soaked, rendering the weapons useless.

Horton's strength was rapidly fading, and he was reluctant to use any of it to pull wet charges and reload the pistols. The Henry and his converted Colts used metallic cartridges that were much less susceptible to moisture, especially when they were waxed where the lead slug and the brass case joined. Horton had done this for as long as he owned the Henry and had never had a misfire because of moisture getting into the powder charge.

"I can't put it off any longer," he said to himself. Lying on his left side, Horton loosened his trousers and inched them down far enough to expose the wounds. He could see that the entrance wound was angry and inflamed around the plug. He could not see the larger exit wound, but he knew that it would be in much the same condition. Horton was only glad that there was an exit wound. He would never have been able to probe for the bullet if it were still in his hip.

He reached over and, without giving himself a chance to hesitate, quickly pulled the cloth plugs, first the one from the exit wound and then the one from near the hip bone. The pain made his vision dim and took his breath away. Horton lay there a moment, exhausted from the pain caused by his efforts. When his vision cleared, he steadied his shaking hands with a drink from his canteen and a pull from the bottle. Then he poured whiskey over the wounds.

It was like pouring molten lead on his flesh. Horton cried out in pain as he slipped back into unconsciousness.

Twice during the next few hours Horton fought his way back to consciousness. The first time was just at dusk. Horton thought that he detected a faint smell of smoke. He found that he still had his right hand on the neck of the bottle. With his left, he fumbled around until he found the cork and then stoppered the bottle. He managed to pull the blankets over himself before he passed out again.

The second time he awoke, it was pitch black. He thought he heard movement, but far off. The noise was like what a man would make if he were riding slowly through brush. Horton put his hand on a pistol and waited. After a while, he drifted off into a deep sleep.

The next time Horton awoke, he felt better. He did not have to fight his way back to consciousness as he had before. He was aware that the sun was well over the horizon and he was grateful for the warmth it provided. He was also conscious of the faint smell of smoke, although the smell was somehow different from the night before. Then he became aware of the smell of fried bacon, and he grabbed for one of the pistols that lay beside him.

"Steady now, Seth," Joe Penbrook drawled soothingly. "Don't you be gettin' yourself in an uproar. "'Bout time you decided to come back an' join the livin'. I was beginnin' to get worried."

Horton groaned and lay back. "I'm glad you're here, Joe," he said, "but how did you find me? I don't even know where I am."

"Just plain dumb luck. Saw your horse runnin' loose without your gear. Figured you'd run into trouble, too, so I set out to find you. Since that horse of yours wasn't near the ranch house, I figured I'd better try the spot where your pa hid him ever' time the cavalry came around lookin' for remounts. That's where you are, about a mile from the ranch headquarters, or what's left of it."

"What's left of it, you say? What happened there?"

"Don't you know, boy? Ain't that how you got shot?"

"If I knew what happened at the ranch, I damn sure wouldn't be trying to get answers from you," Horton said irritably. "Now just what happened back at the ranch?"

"Don't know, exactly. I got back from Gundermann's place after dark. Didn't pass too far from this spot, matter of fact. Anyway, I got to smellin' smoke, an' lots of it, so I sorta scouted around some before ridin' in. I got close enough to see that somebody burned down both barns, the bunkhouse, the outbuildings, and part of the house."

"Did you see anything of the boys?"

"Don't rush me. I was just gettin' to that. Well, I circled around to the ridge to see if our observers was still there. Sure enough, there he was, big as life and twice as dumb. Had a fire goin' big enough to light Austin on a dark night. He was just settin' there, cookin' his hands an' feet at that there big fire. Damn fool. He couldn't of seen ten feet if his life depended on it, which it pretty damned near did. I played with the idea of fetchin' his over the big divide, but decided again' it."

"What stopped you, Joe?"

"Didn't know yet just what went on. If I'd fetched him over, either his body or his not reportin' in might of tipped my hand. Figured I'd find out what happened first, then go back for him if I had to."

"I'm glad you waited. What else did you find out?"

Well, I eased back offa that ridge an' come back up to the house from the west. I didn't just ride in there, in case someone was watchin' from the house. I left my horse in that grove of cottonwoods to the west of the house an' Injuned up to the place. There wasn't no one there. There was a bunch of tracks in the mud, but the rain had about ruined 'em for tellin' what went on. There was a batch of blood on the porch, though. Didn't know whose it was, but after I found you, I figured it was yours. But it ain't, you say?"

"I never made it back to the ranch." Quickly Horton related what had happened in town and what he could remember of his ride.

"If that don't beat all. Looks to me like Delacourte and his bunch musta come lookin' for you at the ranch. When they saw you wasn't there, they burned the place."

"If that's what happened, it's better than even money that the blood you found on the porch is Pepe's. He's a hell of a cook, but I don't think he ever had much call to a real good fighting man."

"I been lookin' over the place this mornin' with a glass, and I ain't seen hide nor hair of Pepe or any of our riders. I didn't see nobody around when I was down there last night, either. Was I to wager, I'd bet that Pepe got croaked an' Delacourte hauled off the body when he was done, just to keep us guessin'."

"You're probably right, Joe, but how could Delacourte hope to get away with this? He must surely know that Watkins will ask questions when he gets back from his trip to Austin."

"I don't rightly know what he plans to say to Watkins, but I seen some riders a little south and a whole lot west of here early this mornin'. "Peered to me they was lookin' for somethin', probably you. I expect that if they was to find us, we'd end up the way of Pepe, or whoever it was who left his blood all over the porch."

"How safe is this place?"

"It'll be good enough for a few days, but sooner or later they'll come across us if they look real hard. That might not happen unless Delacourte or Brannon is leadin' the search in person. The rest of that bunch ain't what you'd call real dedicated. That rain yesterday took care of any tracks we made. If it was me, I'd hole up here 'til I was feelin' better, then go down by the Cowhouse. The country's rough enough down by that creek to hide an army in, as you well know. I'm takin' it that you plan to take this fight back to Delacourte."

"You take it right, Joe. I'll not rest until Delacourte is dead or in jail. I'll fight him as long as there's any life in my body."

"You're a Horton, alright. That there fight might not be as long as you think, though, if we don't get you fixed up some. You poke some of this stuff down your throat an' then I'll take a look at that wound."

Horton took the plate of side meat, biscuits, and beans from Joe. He pulled himself up a little more and leaned back against the blowdown. Joe handed him a cup of coffee and a fork. Horton did not feel much like eating, but his appetite returned after the first few bites. He cleaned the plate and soaked up the grease with the last of the biscuit. When the final crumb was gone, he leaned back and sipped on the coffee.

"Here, this might help you get ready for what comes next," Joe said as he poured an inch of whiskey into Horton's coffee.

"Why is it that I think you're going to enjoy this?" Horton asked, a thin smile creasing his face.

"Well, I'll just tell you. It ain't often that a hired hand gets his boss completely at his mercy. Now supposin' you finish up that coffee while I take a look around for a bit. Then we'll have a try at that hip of yours."

Horton nodded as Joe picked up his rifle and walked off into the mesquite. Horton sipped at his coffee and enjoyed the heat of the liquid and the bite of the whiskey. The food and the whiskey had helped, but he knew he was not out of danger yet. He knew that during the war more than one out of every five men treated for wounds eventually died from them. He felt that this time he did have one major advantage working for him: he was not going to be worked on by an Army surgeon.

Joe came back into Horton's field of vision. "All clear out there, at least for a while. Now let me take a look at what's ailin' you."

Horton rolled onto his left side and winced as Joe probed around the wounds. "You got a nasty lookin' leg there, boy," Joe said, indicating the wound that had nearly cost Horton his life a year ago. "This new addition don't make it no better lookin', either. It's a wonder you didn't bleed to death with no bandagin' or packin' in there."

"That opinion is based on your vast medical experience, I assume," Horton responded.

"Well, I've treated a thousand steers, twice that many horses and mules, and about a hundred damned fools. I expect I can get by with doctorin' one more."

"One more what?"

"Just shut up while I look at this some more." Joe finished his probing, much to Horton's relief.

"You got a pretty good infection goin' in there, boy. I'm going to heat up a section of the cleaning rod from that Henry of yours and run it through the wound. Then I'm goin' to pour what's left of this good whiskey over it and after that I'll bandage whatever's left."

"You're a blood-thirsty old coot," Horton said, grinning at Joe. "Get on with it before I change my mind and let someone who knows what he's doing work on it."

As Joe started to work, Horton thought about Delacourte until the searing kiss of the hot cleaning rode drove his back to unconsciousness.

Chapter 8

Ira Watkins skillfully guided the team of matched dappled gray geldings through Benton's busy main street. The team and the buggy they pulled were the only extravagances he allowed himself, and even after the long trip to Austin and back, he still experienced pleasure in handling such a fine team. He experienced even more pleasure from the admiring glances that the team and rig drew. It was like Ira not to even consider the possibility that a large number of those admiring glances were cast at Sarah, not at the team. To his way of thinking, Sarah was his much-loved daughter, but she certainly posed no serious competition for the grays.

For her part, Sarah was glad to be back in Benton. As much as she hated the shabbiness of the town and the riffraff that Delacourte seemed to attract, she found that at the onset of this trip she was anticipating her return far more than she was looking forward to the prospect of seeing Austin. She also realized that her reluctance to leave Benton and her eagerness to return had more to do with Seth Horton than with any deep ties to the town. She had enjoyed the three days in Austin because of the shopping, the restaurants, and the break from keeping house for her father. She hoped, however, that her next trip would be with Seth.

She blushed slightly at the boldness of her thoughts. Sometimes she worried about how often she found herself thinking about such things. Certainly, her mother would be scandalized if she were alive and knew. Her mother had often preached to her that proper young ladies should think of sex as a wifely duty that corresponded roughly with such things as emptying slop jars, doing laundry, scrubbing floors, and the like. It was sinful to find pleasure in sex, she had often said, and Sarah was fairly certain that her mother had been sinless in this particular area, rest her soul. Poor mama, she thought, and poor papa, too. Guiltily, she turned her thoughts back to the present as Ira pulled the team up in front of their house at the edge of town.

"I'll help you with the packages, but then I got to go to the office. There's no telling what's been going on while we were gone. I may be a while, so don't you go waiting supper on me. I'll be home when I get here."

"Father, you have to take better care of yourself. At least come home to eat. The town has gotten along without you for nearly a week. It can do without you for another night. So can the cafe."

"I didn't get hired to set home, get fat, and sleep my life away. Besides, I don't want the town to figure that they can get along without me. Then I might have to find me a real job." His broad smile and twinkling eyes told Sarah that this little joke meant that she had lost another in a long series of contests with her father's strong sense of duty.

Sarah sighed and started for the house, her arms filled with packages. "You're hopeless. At least try to get home early. Promise?"

"I'll be back as soon as I can," he said, somewhat evasively. "Here, let me get the door for you."

Ira unlocked the door and opened it for Sarah, then went back to the buggy and finished unloading it. When the last package was safely inside, he drove the rig to the livery.

He took his time unharnessing the grays. It was relaxing for him to wipe down the horses and clean the harness. The hostler, an old man known only as Lefty, fed and watered the grays as soon as Ira finished with them. It was a ritual that they had both performed many times before. Ira knew that the next time he came for the rig he would find it cleaned and polished, too. A good man, Lefty, he thought as he left the livery and headed up the street for the cafe. It was close to noon, and he found himself with a fierce appetite.

The cafe was crowded, as usual. Marta Shultz, the owner, was a forty-ish widow of ample proportions who could cook with the angels. Ira had started to pay some attention to Marta after his wife died, but little had come of it. Marta wanted a man with some prospect for reasonable longevity, and being sheriff was not an occupation she viewed as offering such a prospect. For his part, Ira could not see himself as a cafe proprietor. In fact, he could not see himself as anything except a lawman. Still, he and Marta were fond of each other, and on occasion he spent the night at her place. It was a comfortable arrangement for them both. What they considered to be their well-guarded secret was known by nearly everybody in town, including Sarah.

Ira took a seat at the end of the counter as soon as it became vacant. Marta cleared away the dirty dishes and put down a steaming cup of black coffee in front of him.

"It's good to see you back, Ira." She pronounced her 'd's' like 't's.' "I missed you," she said, patting his hand.

Ira looked around furtively to see if anyone had observed this wanton breach of public propriety and, seeing that they were being ignored, smiled back at Marta.

"Missed you, too, Marta. Ain't had a decent meal since I left."

"You flatterer, you. I suppose you want the usual?" she asked as she turned towards the kitchen.

"Of course. Building would probably fall down if I ate anything else. You got any pie left?"

"I got some dried apple pie here, but it's from the last of the apples and I don't think it's real good." Marta sometimes dropped the 'h' from 'th' words, too.

"Save me a piece anyway. The worst pie I ever ate here was wonderful."

Marta returned with a huge steaming bowl of thick stew and a large chunk of fresh bread. In cattle country, the meat was nearly always beef, but from time to time, venison provided a welcome change of pace. This was not one of those times, however. Marta slid a small crock of butter towards Ira.

"You say the sweetest things." Marta lowered her voice to match her eyelids and whispered, "You going to visit me tonight?"

Ira nearly choked on a piece of carrot that seemed determined to go down the wrong way. After a fit of coughing that dislodged the offending vegetable and covered his reddening complexion, he managed to catch his breath. "I will if I get a chance," he responded. "Don't know how much work I got to get caught up with. I ain't been back to the office yet."

"I better not count on you tonight, then. First day you were gone there was a shooting at Jenkins' saloon. That Horton boy and three of Colonel Delacourte's men got into a big fight. They say that Horton killed Ox and Charlie and busted Jock up so bad that Doc says he'll never use his right arm again."

"Damn!" Ira spat. What happened to Horton?"

"I don't know for certain. The bartender said he was hard hit. So did Lefty down at the livery. Horton managed to ride out of town fast enough, though."

"Anything else happen?"

"I hear that Colonel Delacourte has moved some cattle onto the Circle H range. Nobody's seen Horton, Joe Penbrook, or any of his riders since the shooting."

"Damn and double damn!" Ira swore. He hurriedly finished the stew and sopped up the last of the gravy with the bread. "You better hold up on that pie, Marta. I ain't got the time." As he picked up his hat, he said, "Put this on my tab, will you?" His tab had been running for more than four years, and no money had changed hands yet. Neither of them ever expected it to, either. In fact, both would have been insulted if anyone seriously suggested that such a settlement actually be made.

"Of course, Sheriff," she said as he turned and walked rapidly to the door. She was about to say something about later tonight when she thought better of it. Ira would get mad, she knew, and stay away from pure embarrassment. Oh, well, she thought hopefully, maybe he'll be able to come by tonight after all. She moved down the counter to wait on another customer.

The sheriff knew that Delacourte would be at one of three places: his saloon, the bank, or his office up the street from the livery. Ira decided to check them in that order. He set off briskly and finally found Delacourte in his office. Ira walked into the inner office without knocking.

"Oh, it's you, Sheriff. It's about time you got back in town. While you've been off doing God only knows what, that damned Horton fellow has gone crazy and murdered two of my men. I want a warrant sworn out for his arrest, and I demand that you take a posse out looking for him."

"Just hold on there a minute, Delacourte. Far as I can tell you're not sheriff yet, or the judge, either. Even a puffed-up carpetbagger like you ought to know that warrants is issued by a judge."

"It's 'Colonel Delacourte' to you, and we'll see who is sheriff around here after the next election."

"Well, until the election I'm still the man with the star. Suppose you stop tryin' to impress me with how in charge of everything you are an' tell me what Horton is supposed to have done."

"The day you left, Horton rode in here about mid-morning to see me. He said he was having trouble getting the Circle H back on its feet and wanted to know if I'd be interested in taking the ranch off his hands. I offered him a price, quite a generous price I might add, and he accepted. I paid him and he went over to Jenkins' saloon. He got a bottle that he didn't pay for, by the way, and started drinking. Before long, he got pretty loud and some of my men asked him to leave. Horton killed two of them and damned near killed the third. One of my men got a bullet into him before he died. Horton lit out like a scalded cat, probably for Mexico. If he hasn't bled to death, he's probably there by now.

If you hadn't been on vacation, you might have even been able to catch him. You do catch friends of yours, don't you, Sheriff?"

"Don't rightly know, Delacourte. I ain't just been eat up with friends who break the law. I ain't sure that's the case here, either. It's pretty tough to believe that Horton did all those things you accuse him of."

"Are you calling me a liar, Watkins?" Delacourte asked as he rose from behind his desk. "Because if you are, I'll just have to kill you."

"It's 'Sheriff Watkins' to you, an' I'm not callin' you anything, Delacourte. What I'm sayin' is that your story is hard to believe. Now suppose you cool down before I jail you for threatenin' a law officer."

"You? Jail me? You'd have a hard time doing that."

"Maybe so, Delacourte, but your big, bad helper Brannon ain't here to do your fightin' for you, so I just might get the job done after all. You just keep on pushin' and we'll give 'er a try."

Delacourte shot the sheriff a look of pure hatred, but reason penetrated his fury just in time to avert disaster. Delacourte had no doubt that he could kill Watkins, but it would never do to have it known that he had killed him, especially not there in his office. No, if Watkins must die, it should be in some secluded spot with no witnesses. He swallowed his anger and tried to become more cordial to the sheriff.

"You'll have to excuse me, Sheriff. I'm very upset over the murder of my men. In the interest of justice,

I suggest that we not fight with each other over a few words spoken in haste. Please forgive me if I've offended you."

Sheriff Watkins looked at Delacourte with something bordering on astonishment. He thought, brother, that tongue of yours must be hinged in the middle, 'cause it sure 'nuff flaps on both ends. Aloud, he said, "I appreciated that, Delacourte. Supposin' you answer a question or two for me?"

"Whatever you want, as long as it is about the murders. I'm anxious to see justice done in this case."

"Me, too. Now, I suppose you got a bill of sale for the Circle H before handin' that money over to Horton?"

"Of course I did. I'm not stupid."

"I never said you was. Would you show it to me, if it's not too much trouble?"

Delacourte reached into his desk drawer.

"I purely do hope that your hand comes out of there holdin' a piece of paper. I'd sure hate for somebody to get hurt over a misunderstandin'."

Delacourte's hand moved past the Navy Colt and closed over a piece of paper stored in the back of the drawer.

"Here it is, Sheriff. The bill of sale that Horton signed for the Circle H." He handed the paper to Sheriff Watkins.

Watkins studied the paper for a few moments, then spoke. "It's a bill of sale, all right. Can't rightly tell about the signature, though. For now, we'll say that it's Horton's. Did you see this shootin' over at Jenkins' place?"

"No, I didn't. I heard the shots and came out just in time to see Horton ride out of town."

"Then how do you know what happened in the saloon?" Watkins asked.

"I spoke with the bartender and saw the bodies right after it happened. Any fool could figure out what happened."

"Well, this fool is a might slow with figures sometimes. For one thing, it don't figure that Horton would sell the ranch. Things was lookin' up out there an' he still had some cash money left. Got it from you, I heard."

Delacourte reddened at the memory of his first run-in with Horton. "Yes, he got it from me when he paid off the ranch mortgage. What's that got to do with anything? He saw the situation was hopeless and sold out while he had a chance to start over somewhere else."

"Could be, but it don't seem likely. You see, there was five brothers. One got hisself killed with Hood's brigade at Gettysburg. Horton came home to hold the place together 'til the others could get here. That Horton clan is real close an' it ain't like any of 'em to sell the others out for a little money."

"Maybe he planned to split the money with the others. How do I know? He wanted to sell and I bought. It's as simple as that. He went to the saloon, got mean drunk, and murdered my boys."

"That's another thing. I ain't never seen Horton take two drinks at the same settin' as long as I've known him. None of that family drank much."

"You can ask the bartender, if you want. He's the one who told me. Sometimes, Sheriff, being on the losing end of a war changes a man. It has happened to better men than Horton."

Watkins pushed his hat back and scratched his head. "Now I'm real glad you mentioned that. Just so happens that's the third thing that's botherin' me. Seth Horton didn't lose no war. Guess that when your bird dog Brannon was sniffin' around tryin' to find out about the Horton boys nobody saw fit to tell him everythin' about this one. Must be some kind of testimonial as to how well folks around here like you." The sheriff pushed his hat back to its original position and smiled at Delacourte.

"Truth is that four of the Horton boys went off with Hood. The one you picked to tangle with didn't. Seth, now, he was a West Pointer, class of '54 or maybe it was '55. I forget which. Anyway, he stayed in the Union Army when the war started. Was one of them generals when the war finally ended. Served with Phil Sheridan for a good part of the war. Folks in the Army, I'm told, call him 'Wolf.'"

"The man the rebels called 'Lobo?' The same man who won the Medal of Honor as a regimental commander?" Delacourte asked incredulously. He suddenly turned very pale. "My God, it never occurred to me that this was the same Horton."

"That's the man all right. Spent most the whole war commandin' troops. Say, don't I remember hearin' you say that you served on Sheridan's staff durin' the war? Seems to me you should know all about Wolf Horton, seein' how you was workin' for the same man."

"I ... of course I do, but only by reputation," Delacourte said, thinking fast. "You see, I only joined the general's staff very late in the war. Horton was already gone by the time I got there."

"Hmm. I guess it's just bad luck, you two not meetin' before this. Could have saved a lot of trouble, you bein' comrades in arms an' all. Yes, sir, just purely bad luck."

"Who Horton really is, or was, doesn't change what happened here, Sheriff. The man went crazy and murdered two of my men for no cause whatsoever. One man, Charlie Bell, didn't even have a gun on him. I suggest that you talk with the hostler at the livery and the bartender at Jenkins' place. They saw everything I told you."

"Believe I will, Delacourte. An' after I talk to them, I think I'll just drift on out to the Circle H for a little look-see. You don't mind, do you? I mean, you bein' the owner of the place an' all."

"I don't mind a bit. Maybe then we can see justice done for the villainous act."

"I'm all for seein' justice done, an' that's a fact. If you'll excuse me, I'll just walk on over to the livery and talk to old Lefty."

"Of course, Sheriff, of course. Let me know if I can be of any further assistance." Delacourte watched as the sheriff walked out of the inner office. As he opened the front door, Sheriff Watkins nearly collided with Max Brannon.

Brannon stepped aside and let the sheriff pass, then went straight into Delacourte's office. He pulled up a chair and started to roll a smoke from the makings he pulled from a frayed shirt pocket. "What did he want?" Branon asked, jerking his head in the direction of the door through which the sheriff had recently walked.

"We don't have time to go into everything now. I want you to get a couple of the boys and stop the sheriff before he talks to that bartender at Jenkins' saloon. Stop him permanently. While you're at it, get rid of the bartender, too. We can't trust him not to change his story again."

Brannon smiled wickedly. "Be my pleasure, Colonel. That damned tin star's been playin' he-wolf way too long 'round here. Got any idea where he went when he left here?"

"He went over to the livery to talk to the hostler. Now get going. You haven't much time."

"I'm going, an' I'll get Watkins an' that bartender for you. You want I should fetch the hostler, too?"

"No. He didn't see anything I haven't already told the sheriff and several others around town. Just don't miss that sheriff. He could ruin everything we've started here."

"He's dead already. He just ain't fallen over yet. I'll be back directly an' you can fill me in on what happened while he was here."

"Just make sure about the sheriff personally. Without you I don't think the boys can handle him."

"Don't worry none. You really ought to set down for a spell. You don't look too good." Brannon stood up, lit his smoke, and walked out through the outer office onto the boardwalk.

Delacourte sat down heavily behind his desk. He was thoroughly shaken by the sheriff's revelations about Horton. This wasn't just some threadbare ex-rebel soldier with whom he had tangled. This was a Union Army officer, a general, no less, who had considerable influence in Washington and in the Army, should he choose to use it. Delacourte really did know Horton by reputation, and what he knew scared him,

Wolf Horton was known as a fighter who led by example. He was always in the thick of the battle and was known to be tenacious as well as ruthless. His enemies said that he was without mercy, hence the name "Lobo." His men reported that he was a man of great compassion who never asked anyone to do anything that he would not or did not do himself. He was said to be a saint or a devil, depending on whether you fought with him or against him. Delacourte suddenly wished that he had never set eyes on the man.

"Don't panic," Delacourte told himself. "You can still win this game. With the sheriff and that bartender gone, there is nothing to stand in your way. Horton's bound to be rotting out there in the sun."

Somehow Delacourte could not quite convince himself that Horton really was dead. He had been reported dead several times during the war and had always emerged unscathed. Delacourte hoped with all his being that this time Horton would be the loser.

He pulled out his bottom right desk drawer and removed the bottle and a glass that he kept there. Pouring himself three fingers of whiskey into the glass, Delacourte settled back in his chair and tried to relax. "It'll soon be over," he told himself. But doubt still gnawed at the back of his mind.

Chapter 9

Ira Watkins stopped on the boardwalk in front of Delacourte's office and watched Brannon walk into the inner office. Now there's a pair for you, he thought, what mischief one doesn't think of, the other one surely will. He adjusted his hat to a more comfortable position, unhooked the flap on his holster, and moved across the street in the direction of the livery stable. He had little hope of learning anything new from Lefty. Lefty was a quiet man who had achieved old age primarily as a result of being closed-mouthed and making a point of not seeing what went on around him. Folks said Lefty was so dumb he couldn't tell you the time of day. Sheriff Watkins thought it was more a case of Lefty knowing the time but being unwilling to share the information. "Well, it's worth a try," he muttered to himself as he walked down the street towards the building.

The sheriff found Lefty mucking stalls in the rear of the stable. The early afternoon sun shone through the westerly windows, warming the building. The smell of hay, horse, and leather made a pleasant combination, especially to a man like Ira, who had spent most of his life earning a living either on top of a horse or working around them.

"Hello, Lefty," ventured the sheriff tentatively.

"Sheriff." Lefty nodded but did not pause from his work.

"Understand you saw Horton ride out after the shooting last week,"

"Yep."

Ira could see that Lefty was not going to volunteer very much in the way of information.

"What did you see or hear?" he asked, trying to draw Lefty out.

"Heard four shots and a minute later Horton rides in on somebody's horse. Told me to saddle his horse. I did. He got on an' rode out. Colonel Delacourte come out of his place an' let fly with both barrels of his Greener. Didn't hit nuthin', though. Too far away."

The sheriff was amazed. That was more than he had heard Lefty say in the ten years he'd known him. He decided to press his luck and try for more.

"Did you see anything else? Something unusual?"

"Horton was bleedin' pretty good from his right hip. Saddle of that horse he rode in on was fairly covered with blood. The hand holdin' the gun was still steady enough, though."

"What kind of pistol was he holdin'? Could you tell?"

"Yep. It was a Navy Colt."

"Anything else that you remember?"

"Nope."

Lefty's well of knowledge had suddenly gone dry, and the sheriff knew him well enough to know that any further time spent here would be wasted. He thanked Lefty for his help and walked back out of the stable.

Interestin', he thought as he headed down the street towards Jenkins' saloon, Delacourte never said nuthin' about shootin' at Horton. Wonder how he knew it was Horton or that he ought to shoot at him, it bein' kind of dark and rainin' like hell. Wonder where Horton got the Colt Navy, too. Far as I know, he don't own one. Those thoughts and more raced through his mind as he continued down the street.

As he neared the burned-out shell of the church, a man he had never seen before came out from behind the building and hailed him in a low voice.

"Sheriff? Can I talk to you for a minute?"

Watkins let his right hand rest on the butt of his pistol. "What about? Who are you?" he asked.

The name's Smith, John Smith. I seen the Horton shootout. I was there."

"Smith, eh. Seems to me I been meetin' an awful lot of your kin lately. Come out here where I can see you an' we'll talk 'bout what it was you seen."

"I ain't comin' out where Delacourte's crew can see me. They'd bump me off for sure. If you don't want to come back here, just forget about the whole thing. Ain't no skin offen my nose, anyway."

Sheriff Watkins cursed under his breath. He wanted the lowdown on the shootout, but this had the mark of a set-up written all over it. Still, it was broad daylight, and he did not think that anyone would be foolish enough to try something funny before dark. He loosened the Colt in its holster and walked toward the man standing at the rear of the building.

As he stepped past the rear corner of the building, Ira caught a glimpse of movement from the corner of his eye. As he turned towards the movement, he started to draw his Colt. Set up, he thought, and then he felt the crushing blow that struck his head. His world turned black and Ira sank to the ground, unconscious.

"Quick. Help me pull him behind the building," Max Brannon said to Smith as the former dropped the club that he had just used on the sheriff. Together the two men dragged Ira behind the church.

"He dead?" Smith asked.

"Not yet, but he'll make it soon."

Brannon rolled Watkins over on his back with the toe of his boot. Stooping over the sheriff, he drew a knife from its sheath on his belt and cut Ira's throat with a single stroke of the blade.

"That ought to do it," Brannon said as he sprang back to avoid the blood. He wiped his blade on the sheriff's trousers and returned it to its sheath. "We'll have no more trouble from this one."

Retching noise was all the response that Smith was able to make.

"Some bad man you are," Brannon said in disgust. "What you been doing' all this time, stealin' candy from babies?"

"I ain't never done nuthin' like that. You acted like you was butcherin' a hog!" Smith gasped.

"Now, a hog you could eat. That was just gettin' rid of a nuisance. Come on, we got one more to do."

"You ain't plannin' on cuttin' that one, too?" Smith asked hopefully as he stumbled after Brannon.

"Maybe, maybe not. I promise you this, though," Brannon said as he stopped and faced Smith. "If you don't get a hold of yourself real quick, you ain't goin' to be much use to me." He paused a moment to let the words sink in, then continued. "An' if you ain't of use to me, you become a nuisance, too."

Smith paled even more. Those cold eyes of Brannon's told him that he would cut Smith's throat as quickly as he would talk to him. Smith fought down the sudden fear that threatened to choke him.

"Listen, Brannon, you know I'm in this with you all the way. Don't worry about me. I can pull my weight."

"I never worry, Smith, at least not for very long," Brannon said menacingly. "Now let's find that bartender."

Swiftly the men made their way down the alley behind the buildings fronting on the main street. They stopped when they came to the back of Jenkins' saloon.

"I'll go in from the front an' see if he's there. You wait here in case he takes it in his head to leave in a hurry," Brannon instructed.

Smith nodded that he understood and Brannon walked down the side of the building and entered the saloon through the front door. Scanning the room, he saw that the barman he wanted was not there. Pete Jenkins, the owner of the place, was sweeping the floor without much enthusiasm. He leaned the broom against the bar as he prepared to draw the beer that Brannon ordered.

"Strange seein' you here, Jenkins. Where's the regular barman?"

"I haven't the faintest idea. He got his wind up, drew his pay, and left three days ago. Come to think of it, Fred's been spooked ever since Horton killed those men in here last week. Maybe he thought Horton'd come back and finish him, too."

"Maybe," Brannon said. Maybe he figured I'd be comin', he thought. Aloud, he said, "An' you said you got no idea where he went?"

"That's what I said. Why the sudden interest?"

"No special interest. It just seems to me that a lot of strange things been happenin' since this Horton fellow come back. This used to be a peaceful town."

"Depends on how you look at it, I guess. Some folks haven't found it very restful since the war ended."

"Guess you're right," Brannon said. He finished his beer in one long pull and then belched loudly. "See you around, Pete," he said as he flipped a coin onto the bar and walked out the door.

"Thanks for the warning," Jenkins said to himself as he picked up the broom and resumed his sweeping.

Brannon walked carefully around to the back of the saloon. He found Smith facing the rear door, his pistol held in both hands.

"It's me, Smith. Put away the hog leg."

Smith hurried to obey and nearly dropped the pistol in the process.

"Damned if you' ain't graceful. I suppose that if I'd of come through the back door you'd have shot me full of holes." Brannon grabbed Smith by the shirt front. "You got any idea how stupid you looked standin' out here in broad daylight, pointin' a gun at a closed door?"

"You said to get him if he came out the back way. I'd have got him."

"And brought the whole damned town down on our necks. You ain't got much guts, but you got even less brains. Let's get out of here before you hurt yourself."

As they walked back down the alley, Smith asked, "Did you get him? The bartender, I mean."

"Wasn't there. Skipped town three days ago."

Brannon stopped at the mouth of an alley. "You go back to the boys an' I'll report to the colonel. He's goin' to be madder 'n hell about missin' out on the bartender. You try to keep out of trouble. I'm goin' to be keepin' my eye on you."

Smith swallowed hard and nodded. Brannon started walking back up the street towards Delacourte's office. As he walked, he looked at his watch. It had been less than an hour ago that Delacourte had given him his instructions. Now one man lay dead behind the church, and another man was running for his life and no one in town seemed to know or care. He put away his watch and continued on his way to see Delacourte, whistling as he went.

Smith watched Brannon walk away. He turned quickly and nearly knocked down a woman carrying an armload of groceries.

"Watch where you're going, you big oaf!" she hollered at his retreating back.

Smith did not bother to apologize but hurried even faster towards his room. As he went, he thought, that bartender had the right idea. He knew Brannon would come for him sooner or later. Brannon doesn't like me an' I'm the only one who saw him kill the sheriff. Someday Brannon's goin' to come for me, too.

A bolt of fear ran through him, almost causing him to lose control of his bowels.

"I'm leavin' while I can. I ain't cut out for this business anyway," he said to himself as he ran up the steps to his boarding house. Twenty minutes later he was riding out of town, headed south for San Antonio. He never wanted to see or hear of Benton again.

Suppertime came and went. Marta Shultz was disturbed that she had not seen Ira again. It was full dark by the time she had cleaned up the wreckage of the evening meal and laid out what she would need for breakfast the following day. She delayed closing as long as she could. Sometimes Ira would drop by for a late supper and then walk her home. She waited a little longer. Still, Ira did not come. Reluctantly, Marta locked up and went home.

She unlocked the door to her house and went in. Finding a match, she lit a lamp in the kitchen. A bath, she thought, that's just what I need. She started a fire in the stove and heated some water.

Her husband had found Marta's constant desire for bathing somewhat humorous, but because she demanded so little for herself, he had built a small room off the kitchen and had installed a galvanized tin bathing tub in it. Marta had been known to spend an hour soaking in it, especially if her husband or, after his death, Ira were there to scrub her back. Tonight, she filled the tub and then undressed swiftly. Naked, she looked at herself in the mirror.

"Not bad for forty-six," she said appraisingly. She did not look closely at the lines around her eyes or the gray that lately had been attacking her hair more vigorously. The lines and the gray depressed her, even though Ira said that they gave her character. Hard work had kept her figure firm. "Ira, what's keeping you," she murmured as she stepped into the tub.

After her bath, she went upstairs and prepared for bed. She kept expecting to hear Ira's key in the front door, but the only sound she heard was her own breathing. Finally, she turned out the light and went to bed.

"Ira," she said angrily, "you've kept me waiting one night too many." But she knew that she had said the same thing a dozen times before.

A dog, drawn by the smell of blood, stopped to investigate the form lying in the deep shadows of the church. He nosed the still form and, smelling the man smell, ran off into the night. The wind started to blow from the north, and the temperature dropped quickly.

Sarah Watkins Jamison was awakened just after dawn by an insistent knocking at the door. She slipped out of bed, pulled on a robe, and went downstairs.

When she opened the door, she found Mayor Rufus Pflugg standing there, nervously twisting his hat in his hands.

"Miss Sarah, I got some bad news, I'm afraid. Can I come in? It's awful cold out here."

"Of course, Rufus, come in. Can I take your hat?"

"No, thank you, ma'am. I can't stay long. Maybe you had better sit down, ma'am."

A feeling of foreboding gripped Sarah. "I'm fine, Rufus. What is it that you've come to say?"

"Your father's dead, Sarah. There isn't any easy way to say it. Lefty down at the livery found him behind the church as he was going back to the stable after breakfast."

"Oh, my God!" Sarah exclaimed, clutching her throat with her right hand. "How did it happen? When did it happen?" Sarah walked into the parlor and sat down heavily.

"He was murdered, Miss Sarah. It looks like somebody hit him on the head and then ...," he hesitated briefly, "... finished the job with a knife. He'd been lying there a long time, ma'am, since early last night or even before."

"Why would anyone do such a vile thing?" she wailed.

"I don't know, ma'am, but Lefty said that around noon he was asking questions about the Horton shooting. Maybe it had something to do with that."

"Did you say Seth Horton was in a shooting?"

"Yes, Miss Sarah. The day you and your father left for Austin, Seth Horton came to town, sold his ranch to Colonel Delacourte, and then ended up killing two of the colonel's men over at Jenkins' saloon. Lefty saw him ride out of town and says that he was shot hard."

"I can't believe it," Sarah said, shaking her head.

"It's true, ma'am, at least as far as we can tell," the mayor said apologetically.

Sarah pulled herself together and walked over to the mayor. "Here," she said, "give that hat to me. You've nearly twisted the brim off." She took his hat and led him by the arm to a chair. "Please sit down, Rufus. I know that can't be easy for you, either."

The mayor sat in the chair gratefully. Having lost custody of his hat, he began twisting his hands. "Miss Sarah, I don't want you to worry about anything. Doc Waterman is making arrangements for your father, and if you need anything, I hope you'll come to me. After your husband died I always ...," he let his voice trail off. "Perhaps this ain't the time to speak of such things, but ...."

"I appreciate what you're doing, Rufus," Sarah interrupted, "and you're right. This is not the time to speak of such things. Thank you so much for coming to tell me. It was very kind of you. I can manage now, thank you," she said kindly.

Sarah handed his hat to the mayor and led him to the door and let him out. As she closed the door, she found that she could no longer control her emotions.

"Oh, Daddy, why did it have to be you?" she sobbed. She found her way back upstairs and sat down on the edge of her bed. Her feeling of loss was overwhelming.

She felt numb and unfocused. She laid back on the bed and began to cry.

Just before noon, Delacourte and Max Brannon stepped out of the bank and onto the street. Delacourte drew his pistol and fired three shots into the air. A crowd gathered quickly.

"Men," he shouted, "you have all heard of the vicious murder of our esteemed sheriff, Ira Watkins. This foul deed was done while he was investigating the murders of two of my men by Seth Horton. We cannot allow this attack of lawlessness to go unchallenged. With Sheriff Watkins gone, we need a tough, law-abiding man to bring Horton and others like him to justice. I have taken the liberty of appointing the best man I know to that position. That man is Max Brannon. I know that you will all give him your fullest support in bringing the criminal element of this town to justice."

Delacourte holstered his pistol and turned to Brannon. "Sheriff, would you care to say a few words?"

"Thanks, Colonel." Brannon's gaze scanned the crowd. "Starting today, firearms will not be carried inside the town limits by anyone 'ceptin' me an' my deputies." Brannon indicated half a dozen of Delacourte's riders standing in front of the bank, each sporting a star and a shotgun. The crowd began to murmur in protest. Brannon raised his hands into the air.

"Now hear me out. The only way to stop the killin' that's been goin' on is to do away with the weapons. I want all firearms turned into my office. Any man found packin' a gun after sundown today will answer to me, personal. Now let's break this meetin' up." Brannon tipped his hat to Delacourte and walked up the street to the sheriff's office, the newly appointed deputies following closely behind.

Delacourte turned as the crowd began to disburse and walked down the street to his office. Things had gone rather well, he thought. By tomorrow the town would be disarmed and his control could not be effectively challenged.

As he moved down the street, Rufus Pflugg caught up with him. "Colonel Delacourte, what do you mean by this? You have no authority to appoint a sheriff. Only I can do that, with the approval of the town council. You have overstepped yourself, sir."

Delacourte turned and faced the irate mayor. "Rufus," he said, "the last time I checked, I owned this town, at least just about all of it that's worth having. What I don't own, I hold mortgages on. In fact, I hold the mortgage on your house. It's overdue, if you'll remember."

Mayor Pflugg reddened and clenched his fists. "Just what are you saying, Colonel?"

"I'm saying that I own this town, and you, lock, stock, and barrel. I can do anything I want to do, and that includes appointing a sheriff or even a mayor. If you don't believe me, I suggest that you try giving me a challenge."

"You can't get away with this, Delacourte!" Pflugg sputtered angrily. "The people won't stand for it."

"I already have gotten away with it, Mister Mayor, and the people will stand for whatever I tell them. Now, I've had enough of you," he said menacingly. "If you want to keep your job and your easy life here, you'll go back to your office and behave yourself. Now leave me alone. I have important things to do."

The two men glared at each other. Pflugg broke his gaze away and, looking deflated, walked back up the street. Delacourte smiled and resumed walking toward his office. He was whistling by the time he reached the door. He found Sarah waiting for him in the outer office.

"Why, Miss Sarah," he said as he bowed slightly and removed his hat. "What an unexpected pleasure. Please accept my sincere condolences over the foul murder of your father. Rest assured that I will leave no stone unturned in my hunt for the villainous killer."

"You need not look much farther, Mr. Delacourte. He's in the jail now," she responded with anger.

"It's 'Colonel,'" he said coolly. "You mean to say that they've caught the man?"

"No, I mean that you have appointed him. Max Brannon killed my father, and probably on your order. My father was the only man who stood between you and the total control of this town once you had Seth Horton shot. Max Brannon and you are the foul villains, sir!"

Delacourte put down his hat and turned back to Sarah. "Missus Jamison, you have made some very serious charges, all of which are without basis, I assure you. I'll make allowances for the fact that you are distraught by your grief and don't know what you're saying."

"I know perfectly well what I'm saying, and you know what I'm saying is true. I just can't prove it."

"You can't prove it because it isn't true."

"Liar!" she spat.

"Have it your way, Missus Jamison. Take all the time you need to get your affairs in order before you leave town."

"I have no intention of leaving town, Mister Delacourte."

"You may not intend to leave now, my dear, but make no mistake; leave you will. If you choose to stay, you can move in with me. I suppose I can convince Myrna to go back to the cribs at Fat Ethyl's. Maybe I'll keep you both, if you behave yourselves."

Sarah's face flamed. "You unspeakable animal," she hissed. "You're worse than a murderer. You are a man without any sense of decency or honor."

Delacourte laughed, then lowered his voice and narrowed his eyes menacingly. He spoke quietly but forcefully. "I can't afford those luxuries. Now hear me: I've said all that I'm going to say. Leave town on your own or I'll put you out. Permanently."

Sarah replied with similar force. "Don't you dare threaten me, Mister Delacourte, or whoever you are. I intend to stay and you and your thugs can't run me out. There will be justice done here, Mister Delacourte. You can count on it!" With that, Sarah turned and left the office, slamming the door as she went.

Delacourte smiled. She might make a pleasant diversion after all, he thought, Myrna is beginning to bore me. This little spitfire would be a pleasure to tame.

Sarah gradually gained control over her fury as she walked up the street. As she neared the cafe, she suddenly thought of Marta and of the long-standing relationship she had shared with her father. Sarah decided to stop and see if Marta needed any help or comfort.

As she neared the door, she saw a sign announcing that the cafe was closed until further notice. Sarah hurried up the street, pausing only once to catch her breath. She ran up the steps of Marta's house and knocked loudly on the door. Hearing no response, Sarah knocked again and then again. Finally, Marta answered the door, tear stained and disheveled, with a Colt pocket pistol in her hand.

"Marta! Is somebody after you?" Sarah asked.

"No," answered Marta slowly. "I am going to join my Ira."

"Oh, Marta, you can't! That won't help my father!"

"Maybe not. I don't know. I just don't have anything more to live for now that your father is gone."

"But you do, Marta! I need your help if we are ever going to see his killer brought to justice." Sarah reached out and took the pistol from Marta's yielding fingers.

"How? How can I help?" Marta asked, looking up with a spark of hope into Sarah's eyes.

"If you'll let me come in, I'm sure that we can think of something."

Marta nodded and opened the door wider to allow Sarah to pass. Sarah closed the door firmly behind her.

Chapter 10

Horton felt the heat from the early April sun and tried for the hundredth time to control his increasing restlessness. It had been more than two weeks since his run-in with Ox and Charlie at Jenkins' saloon and he was eager to take the fight to Delacourte. He had heeded Joe Penbrook's advice to stay in hiding until his wounds healed and his strength returned, but hiding was not in his nature. He was far more accustomed to leading a charge than hiding in a hollow. He longed for activity as some men long for strong drink or gold. Now that Horton's wounds were nearly healed, Joe was finding it more and more difficult to keep in him camp.

He and Joe had been in this camp for twelve days. Three days after Joe found him in the draw, the foreman rigged a travois and moved Horton to a place along the Cowhouse Creek known as Wallow Hollow. There, erosion had carved deep gouges in the earth, and the draws and hollows were filled with cottonwoods, cedar, and mesquite trees. Staying well back from the creek in order to avoid any danger from flash flooding, the two men had waited for Horton to regain his strength before they launched their campaign to bring Delacourte and his crew to account for the murder of Pepe Mendoza.

They both knew it had been Pepe who had died on the porch of the Circle H ranch house. Seth and Joe had found the shallow grave containing Pepe's body while moving to their present camp. Finding the body had removed from Horton's mind the last reservations about declaring war on Delacourte. Until that moment, there had still lingered in his mind the possibility that the fight at Jenkins' might have been a spontaneous thing, not a premeditated attempt to kill him. Now Horton knew for a certainty that either he or Delacourte would have to die before this fight was over.

Horton had not wanted a fight in the beginning. All he had wanted was to escape from his memories of war and have a chance to see his family again. That his family was not here was not the fault of Delacourte. The constant pressure to buy or drive Horton from his land was, however. Horton knew that he had had enough, both of Delacourte and of waiting.

Getting to his feet, he moved to the lip of the hollow, where Joe Penbrook was keeping watch.

"What are you doing up here now? Ain't your turn to watch for at least another hour."

"I know, Joe. I can't stand this waiting any longer. I'm healed up enough not to leave a trail when I move. That's good enough. It's time we started hurting Delacourte."

"Think you're ready to fight, do you? How do you think you're goin' to ride? Why, you weren't even able to stand up by yourself 'til a few days ago. A sick dwarf could whip you in less than a minute."

"Maybe you're right, Joe, but I wasn't thinking of standing up in a toe-to-toe fight with Delacourte. I was thinking more about striking at the edges of Delacourte's operation, cutting deep when we can, scratching when we can't. Sooner or later, he'll end up bleeding to death. That won't happen while we're sitting here starving to death on your lousy cooking."

"It may be lousy, but it's done alright by you. You seem to be back to your old sassy self. I liked you better when you was sick and silent," Joe responded, the corners of his mouth twitching in a losing effort to restrain a smile. "Next time you get your butt blowed off, I ain't goin' to be so quick to fix you up."

"Probably won't happen again. There isn't much of a target left on that side anymore."

Joe hawked and spat. "This idea you got to go chewin' around Delacourte's edges sure has the smell of wolf tactics to it. You bein' called Wolf an' all, I guess maybe we had better get started. Got anything particular in mind?"

"First thing I need to do is get back to the ranch. We are going to need some money and I'm betting that Delacourte and his bunch haven't found the stash in the fireplace. Next, I need to see Ira Watkins. If we can settle this within the law, we will."

"What if we can't?" asked Joe.

"Then we'll settle it any way we can. In this fight, Delacourte has actually done us a favor. By destroying the Circle H headquarters, he has eliminated any need for us to defend anything. That leaves us free to hit him when and where we want. If we're careful, he's got practically no chance of catching us."

"Sounds like you ain't expectin' the law to help."

"I don't know how much Ira can do. We've got no witnesses to Pepe's murder and no proof that Delacourte sent that bunch after me. A lot will probably depend on what Delacourte's done in the last two weeks and how badly we can get him rattled. I think he's the type to act rashly and make mistakes when he's angry or afraid."

"When are we goin' up to the ranch?" Joe asked.

"Not 'we,' Joe. Me. I'd like you to get rid of that observer, if he's still there. I'm going to have to ride most of the way to the house, I'm afraid, and I don't want him alerting Delacourte right away."

"You want him gone permanent?"

"I'd rather not kill anyone else if we can get the law to take care of Delacourte. Another body would confuse the issue. They change the guard around noon, if they are still following the same pattern. I'll just plan on riding in a couple of hours later. After I get some money, I'll ride to town and see Ira after dark. When you get done with the observer, come back and move camp about a mile upstream. There's a good spot there right about where my brother Marcus broke his leg when we were boys."

"I know the spot. Anythin' else?"

"If anything goes wrong, we'll meet at the new site as soon as we can or leave a message there about where we can be found. Anytime we both leave a camp, we never go back to it. That way, if somebody finds it while we're gone, we won't ride back into an ambush."

"Good. Now tell me, Mister General Wolf, are you goin' to catch your own horse, or is ol' Private Penbrook goin' to do it for you?"

Horton laughed. "The Wolf would be honored if Mister Penbrook would select his steed."

"An' while I'm at it, I'll get your horse, too," Joe said. "I swear. Four years of education at government expense an' you still can't talk American." Joe flipped Horton a salute and went down into the hollow to get his horse, leaving Horton to keep watch. The boy's plenty game, Joe thought. I hope it's enough.

Penbrook decided to make one more sweep of the ridge. For more than an hour he had been looking for one of Delacourte's observers, but all that he had found were old sites. Time was running out for him. In less than an hour, Seth would be riding up to the ranch house. If he hadn't found the observer by then, it could spell big trouble for Horton.

Abruptly he came upon a site that had been used recently. Joe dismounted and studied the site.

"Two men," he said softly. "One man who stayed here for a while and a second one that joined him not too long ago." Joe saw that the sides of the hoof prints had not yet started to crumble and that the prints had been made after the sun had burned the heavy dew from the ground. Probably moved out sometime in the last hour or two, he thought.

Joe mounted his horse and followed the tracks as far as he could and still remain hidden. The tracks led directly to the Circle H ranch house.

"I sure hope Seth remembers what he's been taught and keeps his eyes open," he muttered to himself. There was no question but what the ranch house was occupied, at least temporarily, by at least two of Delacourte's riders.

Shortly after two o'clock, Horton eased the big bay among the cottonwoods just west of the ranch house. He stopped just inside the wood line and carefully observed the ruins of the ranch headquarters. He quickly spotted the two horses tied in front of the house. As he watched, he saw two men emerge from the building and stand on the porch. Horton took his binoculars from his saddlebags and took a closer look at the pair. When the figures came into focus, Horton recognized

Brannon but not the second man. What he did recognize was the gleam of a lawman's badge on the chest of each man.

Horton's thoughts raced. He knew that Ira Watkins would never consent to having Brannon or any other man from Delacourte's crew serve as a deputy. That these men were wearing badges meant that Ira was no longer the law in Benton. Horton could not believe that Watkins would give up the badge of his own free will. That meant that the badge probably had been taken from his body and that nothing or no one stood in Delacourte's way except for Joe and himself. Horton watched as the men mounted and rode away.

He waited in the grove for several minutes before riding up to the house. He nearly fell as he dismounted. His right hip was still stiff and very sore. He limped into the house and surveyed the damage. All the furniture was broken up or burned. Smoke stained the walls and ceiling, but the basic structure was still sound. He saw several signs that small animals had already taken over the house.

He walked into the kitchen and found that Joe's reports had been correct. More than half of the ceiling and roof were burned, but there was little damage to the walls. The burned remains of Joe's Sharps .50 were in the corner by the stove. Walking out onto the porch, Horton saw the dark stains that he knew were Pepe's blood. He also saw two holes in the boards near the center of the stain. Pepe had been shot as he laid there, he decided. Horton no longer felt a need to work within the law, especially since the law now appeared to be Delacourte.

Horton went back through the kitchen and into the front room. He walked to the fireplace, moved the grates to one side, and stooped to remove a tightly fitted stone from the floor of the firebox. He quickly extracted a small metal box from the hole. Opening the box, Horton removed twenty gold double eagles and then returned the box to its hiding place. After he replaced the stone and the grates, he spread ashes to cover any signs of his having been there. Horton moved as quickly as he could through the front door and mounted his horse. He thought for a moment and then turned the horse away from the house and headed toward Benton.

As Horton rode, he saw that several hundred head of cattle had been moved onto the Circle H range. He moved towards one group and got close enough to identify the brand.

"The Circle J Bar D," he said to himself. "I'd sure like to see the underside of that hide." He was sure that he would find that the original brand had been the Circle H. He decided that the next time he and Joe needed some camp meat, he'd find out for sure.

Horton had planned to go directly to the sheriff's office when he reached Benton. Now that he knew Brannon was there, he decided to go to Sarah's house instead. Depending on what he learned from her, he would decide whether to open his war on Delacourte immediately or rejoin Joe to plan a strategy. He knew that he needed to retain a degree of flexibility because he had no way of obtaining information about Delacourte before he reached town. He wished that he had some of the men from his old regiment with him. If they were here, the Delacourte problem would be gone before sunset. As it was, Horton feared that the war would be a long and, no doubt, bloody one.

Horton drew rein near the crest of the knoll overlooking the west side of town shortly after dark. The Watkins house was situated off the main street near the edge of town. It would be an easy matter for him to leave his horse concealed among the trees and work his way down to the house unobserved. Horton dismounted and tied the big bay loosely to a mesquite branch. Moving slowly to favor his right leg, he edged cautiously down the hill, up the steps to the back door of the Watkins house, and rapped gently on the door. A few moments later he heard Sarah on the other side of the door.

"Who's there?" she asked hesitantly.

"It's me, Seth," he responded.

A moment later the door was flung open and Sarah was in his arms, nearly knocking him from his feet.

"Oh, Seth," she breathed, "I was afraid that you were dead. I was so worried! She held him tighter, then kissed him fiercely.

Horton disengaged himself from Sarah with some difficulty and said, "As much as I enjoyed that, I'd like to come in before Brannon or Delacourte sees me. I don't think I'm too popular with either of them right now."

"Oh, I never thought ...."

"I just have to be careful, Sarah. I don't have many friends in town," he said as he moved past her into the room. As she closed the door behind him, he asked, "Are you alright?"

"They killed Daddy, Seth. They killed him and left him lying in the dirt. Then Delacourte made Brannon sheriff. They've taken over the town and everything in it."

"I thought that might be the case. This afternoon I saw Brannon and one of his deputies at the Circle H. I knew your father never would have hired them. I'm sorry about your father, Sarah. He was a good man."

"I was so worried about you, Seth. Mayor Pflugg told me you had been shot and that you'd sold the ranch to Delacourte. When no one heard from you for two weeks, I was afraid that you might be dead, too."

"I nearly was. I never sold the ranch. After the fight with Delacourte's boys, Joe Penbrook found me and doctored me until I could take care of myself. I'm still a little shaky. Do you mind if I sit down somewhere?"

She guided him into the parlor and sat down next to him. "What are we going to do now, Seth?"

"I don't really know. I came here tonight to find out what's been going on here so I could plan an attack on Delacourte."

"I can help you. So can Marta Shultz. We were going to try something on our own if you were …," her voice trailed off.

"Joe and I can use all the help we can get. We need to know where Delacourte spends his time, how many men he has working for him, and anything else that we could use to find a way to get at him."

"Marta and I'll get whatever you want. How will we get it to you?"

"I can't come in very often, Sarah. They may be watching you as it is. Suppose I meet you at Marta's a week from now?"

"Must it be so long?"

"I'm afraid so. I need the time to get stronger. I still can't walk very far, and running is completely out of the question. I'd rather wait and beat Delacourte than hurry and lose."

"Of course," she said. "I was being selfish. I just wanted to see you and be with you."

And with that, Sarah leaned over and kissed him again, softly. This time he did not attempt to cut the embrace short. Finally, they parted.

"This is serious," he said.

"It certainly is," she replied breathlessly.

"And we can't let it get any more serious until Delacourte has been brought to justice. There is too much for which he must answer. Nothing must stand in the way of that, Sarah, not even us."

"Is there ever going to be an 'us,' Seth?" she asked.

"I honestly don't know. Three weeks ago, I thought there might be. When this is over, perhaps there will be. Until then, we can't even consider it."

"Whatever you say is what I'll do, Seth."

They sat in silence for a few moments and then Horton slowly got to his feet. He told Sarah the specific things he needed to know. He also gave her some of the money he had taken from the ranch so that she could pay for the equipment he needed. She nodded in understanding and walked with him to the door, turning out the lamp before she opened it.

"No light, no silhouette," she whispered.

"You'd make a fine trooper," he said, smiling. "I'll see you next week at Marta's."

He slipped out of the door and worked his way cautiously back to his horse. Mounting, he rode slowly west and then turned south. The sun was just breaking the horizon when he rode into camp.

On the same evening, three men sat around a table in the Silver Star Saloon in Pueblo, Colorado Territory. They were gaunt and bearded, dressed in remnants of Confederate gray and well-worn miner's clothing. They were tired men, used to hard work as well as danger.

Each was armed with a knife and a pair of Colt 1851 Navys. The man who appeared to be the oldest of the three was shuffling a deck of greasy cards. The other two were waiting patiently for him to finish.

"Jim, how far you reckon we come?" the man with the cards asked as he began to deal.

"Well, Marcus, I guess we're about halfway there. Another ten or twelve days should see us home if we don't run across anything to slow us up. What's your guess, Matt?"

The youngest of the three nodded in agreement. "That's how I got it figured, too. Can't be too soon for me, either. We been gone way too long."

The other two murmured in agreement. Once the cards were dealt, the play of the hand proceeded quickly. The men played only for diversion and no money was on the table. Running totals of fortunes won or lost in these games were kept in the memory of each man. Accuracy was not a concern, since no one expected the debts to be paid anyway.

The men sat at the table quietly playing cards and drinking sparingly for two hours or more as the saloon started filling up. By ten o'clock the place was noisy and smoke-filled, with men standing two-deep at the bar, drinking freely. A tall, thin man with a saloon pallor and holding a half-filled glass of beer in his hand walked over to the table.

"You mind if I set in?" he asked hopefully.

"We ain't playin' for money, mister. If you're lookin' to win a stake, you come to the wrong place," the man called Marcus answered. It was plain that he spoke for the group.

"That's fine by me. I can't afford to lose, anyway. Fact is, I really just want a place to sit and maybe have a little conversation. I'm plumb wore out from travelin'."

"Know how you feel," Jim said. "We been travelin' quite a spell, too."

"You come from the Colorado gold fields?" the stranger asked.

"Yeah, the Dakotas, too. An' you?" Matt asked.

"I just left a dried-up hellhole called Benton down towards Austin. Name's Fred Handlemann. Used to be a barman there." He offered his hand to each of the men at the table. They shook it in turn and gave their Christian names.

"So, you just come in from Benton," said Marcus. "We heard of the place. How come you left?"

Well, it's kind of a long story. If you really want to hear it, I'll tell it. If you don't, just say so."

Assured by the three that they wanted to hear it, Handlemann related his experiences in the town and ended with the shootout at Jenkins' saloon. He paused only once to drink from his glass. When he finished, he leaned back in his chair.

"I figured it was only a matter of time before Delacourte sent Brannon after me or I got to be the victim of an accident or somethin', so I lit out of there quick as I could. Figure I'll try the gold fields you just left."

The other three men looked at each other and Marcus scooped up the cards on the table. "Reckon we better be gettin' some sleep. We got a long, hard ride ahead of us tomorrow. How long did it take you to get here, Mister Handlemann?"

"Been riding' hard for eleven days. Why?"

"'Cause we're headin' for Benton," Marcus answered.

"Same question. Why? You must have an awful good reason after I told you what's goin' on there."

Marcus smiled coldly at him. "Last name's Horton. Is that reason enough?"

Fred Handlemann finished the last of his beer and wiped his mouth on his sleeve. "Yes, sir. I reckon that it is. I reckon that it's more than reason enough. I wish you a lot of luck. You're goin' to need it."

Chapter 11

Seth Horton woke to the smell of frying bacon. He groaned and rolled onto his back, opening one eye as he did. Joe looked up from his cooking and shook his head sadly.

"Glad to see you're back with the livin'. You've damn near slept the day away. Sun'll break over the rim 'most any minute now, so you better get up. This here hotel don't have no room service."

Horton smiled, threw back his blanket, and sat up. "And a good morning to you, too, Mister Penbrook. Is the coffee done?"

"Been done for an hour," he snorted. "That Yankee army just plain spoilt you. Got you into the habit of sleepin' 'til noon an' expectin' somebody to wait on you. A hell of a thing to have happen to what used to pass for a Texan."

"You're right, Joe. I can tell you, though, that my aide used to be a lot less sassy and a hell of a lot better looking."

"What was 'er's name, Fat Ethyl?" Joe countered.

"I give up. You're incorrigible."

"Don't know about that, but since it's a cinch I ain't gonna change any time soon."

Horton laughed and Joe joined in. In many ways, these days of waiting to start the campaign against Delacourte had been good ones. The six days since he had returned from town had passed swiftly. Joe had proven himself to be a better than average tactician and had offered many suggestions that Horton had found useful in completing his plan. Tonight, they would start to put their plan into action.

After they had eaten, the men cleaned the plates and began to break camp. It would be important for them to keep on the move after tonight. Earlier in the week, Joe had ridden into Austin with two messages, one for the military commander in Austin and one for General Sheridan. In both, Horton had outlined what had happened in Benton, and he had suggested that an outside law agency be sent to take charge of the situation. To Sheridan he had outlined the concept of the plan he intended to follow if no assistance from the law was forthcoming.

Horton really had no expectations that any assistance would be available. Military units and law agencies were stretched far too thin across the frontier to meet a fraction of the demands made for their help. Most frequently the only justice a man could expect came from the muzzle of his gun. The men knew the rules and accepted them. This was Horton's fight and he was prepared to fight it. The messages were a formality to protect the military. The one sent to Sheridan had suggested the immediate acceptance of Horton's resignation should the outcome of the battle go against him

Basically, the plan that he and Joe had devised was to isolate Delacourte and his men from their base of support, the town. It was their intention to drive Delacourte into the open and force him to defend one particular area, in this case, the Rafter T. There, Seth and Joe could pick away at Delacourte's crew as the opportunities presented themselves until the stronghold was weak enough to be attacked directly. That the plan had a great many holes was understood and accepted. It was designed to accept revision as the changing situation demanded. The key to the plan's success was the isolation of Delacourte. Without a base of support, Delacourte was vulnerable. Horton also wanted to move the fight well away from the town, so that innocent people were less likely to get hurt.

As he looked for his own vulnerable areas, Horton could find only two: the size of his force and Sarah. His concern for her, he knew, was his greatest weakness. On the frontier, good women were treated with respect bordering on reverence. The quickest way to get hung was to harm one.

Usually, Horton would have been willing to rely upon this code for the protection of Sarah, but Delacourte would follow no code or convention if it stood between him and success. Sarah's safety must be assured if Horton was to have the freedom of action he needed to make his plan succeed.

About his other weakness, Horton was not particularly concerned. Either he and Joe would be enough to do the job, or they would fail. In this case, failure would mean death. The only consequence that he would be alive to deal with was winning. Horton dismissed all thoughts of losing from his mind.

Darkness found Horton and Joe on the outskirts of town. Both men were dressed in dark clothing to help them blend into the shadows. For the attack tonight, they had discarded their heavy boots in favor of moccasins, in case there was a need for stealth. The night was cloudy and a strong wind had sprung up that would mask what little noise they might make. They had moved cautiously into a position overlooking both the cafe and Marta's house so that they could time their arrival for after Marta's return. There was little activity in the streets, and they were unable to spot any signs of obvious danger. Horton continued to watch carefully. The one thing he did not was to do tonight was walk into the waiting arms of Max Brannon and his deputies.

The minutes seemed to pass like hours as they waited in the darkness. Finally, the lights in the cafe flickered out. Horton waited impatiently for a few more minutes and then nudged Joe. It was time to go. The familiar feeling of excitement surged through Horton as he silently glided through the shadows, moving swiftly towards Marta's. They were committed now. The battle would be joined tonight.

When they reached Marta's house, they saw only a single light in an upstairs room. Cautiously Seth tapped on the door, which was opened immediately by Marta.

"Come in quickly," she whispered. "Sarah is already here." She closed the door after they both had entered and then led them into the bathroom.

"We can talk better in here," she said. "There are no windows to show the light or to listen through." A lamp in the corner was turned up enough to cast a dim light over the room. Sarah moved away from the lamp and crossed the room to Seth.

"I'm so glad you made it safely. Has there been any trouble?" she asked.

"None," replied Horton. "It's almost as though they don't believe that we're alive. There is nobody watching the Circle H any longer, and we couldn't see even a single deputy on patrol. I don't think I've ever seen the town so quiet."

"Brannon and his deputies, they think you are dead," Marta responded. "The town is quiet because so many people have left in the past two weeks. Those that stayed on keep off the streets at night for fear of Brannon's men."

"How many men do Delacourte and Brannon have now?" Joe asked.

Sarah answered quickly. "Brannon keeps six gunmen as his deputies. They control what happens in town.

During the day, there is at least one of them at the bank and two more with Colonel Delacourte. At night they stay at the jail, except for the two who stand guard at Delacourte's house. I understand that there are another ten or twelve men at the Rafter T, but those are mostly to work the ranch. How many would be willing to fight for Delacourte, I don't know. In addition to the deputies in town, there are five men who run businesses for the Colonel. I don't know if they'll fight, either."

"We do know that there are eight men counting Delacourte in town who will fight. We'll try to cut that down some tonight," Horton explained. "We're going to try to panic Delacourte enough to get him and his gunmen to move out to the Rafter T. I want Delacourte alive so that a judge can have him hung legally. I'm afraid that if we try to take him in town there may be a lot of innocent people who get hurt. Sarah, were you able to find out about the explosives?"

"Yes. Tad Beckley at the general store keeps some in his back room, along with fuses and other things. Mister McAmis at the colonel's store does, too. I don't know how much you want, but I don't think that either store has very much. Tad has the rifles you asked me to find out about. One has a glass sight."

Horton was pleased to hear this. He wanted a long-range sniping rifle for Joe and himself. His Henry would throw a 200-grain slug accurately up to two hundred yards, but the 26-grain powder charge was not enough for much accuracy beyond that range. He had asked Sarah to locate at least one Sharps .50 if she could. Apparently, she had. The telescopic sight was a real bonus. It would permit precision shooting at greater ranges than an iron sight would.

"Good!" Joe interrupted. "One shot from one of them would derail a train at a mile or trim the eyebrows off a jackass at half that range. Better save the one with the fancy sight for yourself, boss. I don't need them new-fangled magnifyin' things."

Horton nodded. "Actually, I'd prefer the telescopic sight as long as the glass doesn't fog. We used them with good effect during the war. I'm sure we'll find it useful here, too.

Horton turned to Sarah and said, "I'm going to plant a charge at the bank while Joe puts one at Delacourte's office, providing that there's enough powder to take care of it and the jail, too. While everybody's busy inspecting the damage, I'm going to pay a visit to Delacourte. If I can get to him then, I'll take him to Austin for trial. If I can't, we'll proceed with the basic plan to make him hole up at the Rafter T. Whatever happens, I want you and Marta to leave town right now."

"I can't do that," Marta protested. "I have a business to run. Besides, I can help. I can use a rifle as good as any man."

"So can I," Sarah added. She, too, was unhappy at being asked to leave town.

"I'm sure you can, both of you. But if Delacourte decides that you're in on this, I'm afraid he might use you to get at us. Everybody knows I was seeing you before this thing broke wide open. It won't take Delacourte long to take advantage of that, even if he doesn't know you've had anything to do with what we're going to do tonight."

"We'd never tell him anything. We really don't know anything that would be useful to him once the explosions take place," Sarah responded.

"He could hold you hostage. That would limit what Joe and I could do. He could also kill you in a fit of rage, to hit back at me."

"He wouldn't dare harm us!" Marta said indignantly. "Nobody would dare to harm a woman!"

"I'm afraid that Delacourte isn't like most men," Horton reasoned. "There is no telling what he'll do when he's pushed. He's like a rabid dog—totally unpredictable and mean clear through."

"Well, I'm not going," Sarah said firmly. "I can take care of myself. Marta can, too."

"Do you realize that if Delacourte gets his hands on you it could cost Joe and me our lives?" Seth asked angrily.

Sarah sobered. "I didn't think of that. I was only thinking about how Marta and I could handle any danger to ourselves."

"I have asked you to leave. If you choose to ignore my request to leave and you fall into Delacourte's hands, I may not be able to help you. You'll just have to take your chances like the rest of us," Horton said, looking her straight in the eyes.

Sarah's gaze never wavered. "That's fine with me," she said coldly. She turned to Marta. Marta spoke before Sarah could ask the obvious question. "It's fine with me, too."

Horton shook his head in resignation. He had commanded a division in combat but could not get two women to follow his orders. "I don't like it," he said. "At least stay together. You can protect each other better that way."

Finally, everyone agreed on the compromise, although the atmosphere in the room was still decidedly cool. Sarah turned the lamp very low so that the men's eyes could adjust to the dark. A few minutes later Seth and Joe slipped back into the night.

Joe and Horton kept to the shadows as they moved cautiously down the alleys to Tad Beckley's general store. Upon reaching the back of the building, Horton sent Joe around to the side while he forced the back door. The lock proved to be an old one, and in a matter of moments Horton was inside the back room looking for the explosives. He found a lantern and lit it, keeping the flame very low. Horton worked his way through the crates and stacks of merchandise stored in the room until he finally found a narrow door marked, "Explosives." There was a padlock on the door. Horton retraced his steps and went into the main part of the store. Shielding the dim light as best he could, he quickly found the Sharps rifles and three hundred rounds of ammunition. Those he moved to a handy spot by the rear door. Returning to the main store, Horton left five gold double eagles on the counter, picked up a pry bar, and returned to the powder room. It took him only a minute or two before he had the door open and he was able to enter the room.

In contrast to the clutter of the back room, the powder room was very orderly. It was plain that Tad Beckley cleaned the floor daily. All kegs leaked, and it would only take a little black powder ground under a boot heel to set off all the powder in the room. Horton was glad he was wearing soft moccasins which practically eliminated all chance of an accident of that sort. Quickly, he removed the eight kegs of black powder he found, along with several coils of slow fuse. As he was about to leave the powder room for the last time, Horton spotted a packing case in the far corner. Opening the lid, he found a number of small, glass-stoppered bottles resting deeply in a bed of sawdust and cotton.

"Nitro, by God!" he exclaimed. Nitroglycerin had only become available three years before. This highly explosive liquid was very unstable and required delicate handling. For that reason, very little of the substance was to be found on the frontier. By Horton's way of thinking, only a man with a death wish would haul the stuff.

Horton felt a cold draft on his neck. Turning quickly, his hand flashed toward the Colt on his hip. It was only at the last split second that he recognized the shadowy figure in the doorway.

"Wondered what was takin' you so long. Thought you might of went to sleep in here," Joe drawled.

"Don't ever sneak up behind me again, Joe. You came pretty close to scaring yourself to death."

"I wasn't scared none."

"Maybe not, but I was," Horton said as he stepped into the beam of light and eased the hammer forward on his pistol.

"I see what you mean," Joe said softly as he watched Horton holster the pistol. "We ready to get goin'?"

"We are. The powder, fuse, and the Sharps are by the back door. Suppose you take the rifles and as much of that ammunition as you can carry back to the horses while I start setting the charges at the bank. Sarah said that the side door is kept barred and I don't want to chance breaking in through the front. I'm going to try to blow out the side wall instead. That should put the place out of business for quite a while."

Joe nodded. "We got enough powder for Delacourte's office, too?"

"I think so. When you get back from the horses, take two of the kegs of powder and the fuse I'll leave outside and plant them well under the building. Since the place is built on piles, you shouldn't have much trouble."

"Lessen I meet a snake under there, I won't. If I do find one, the whole town will likely know about it."

"Do what you think is best. That fuse is supposed to burn at the rate of one foot a minute. Cut about thirty feet of it and light it at half an hour before midnight. That'll give you time enough to take the other two kegs and set them at the rear of the jail. You might cut that fuse so it'll go off a little before midnight, but just a little. When the charges go off, I'll try to go in after Delacourte in the confusion."

"I know the plan," Joe said a little testily. "Come daylight, I'll be on the ridge overlookin' Rafter T pot shootin' anythin' that even looks like it's comin' to town."

"Good. I'll meet you there as soon as I can, with or without Delacourte. If I can get him, we'll all go into Austin from there."

Both men set about completing their work. Horton took a shovel from the storeroom and, as quietly as he could, dug a trench along the side of the bank large enough to hold the four kegs of powder. Once the kegs were in position, he cut two fuses, one for each keg to eliminate the chance of some flaw in the fuse preventing the explosion. When the fuses were ready, Horton shoveled dirt back over the kegs and then placed several bottles of nitroglycerin carefully on the dirt over the powder. The bank was practically the only brick building in town, and he wanted to make sure he damaged the place enough to make it useless to Delacourte. To prevent someone from breaking into the bank through the walls of buildings on either side, the lots on both sides of the bank had been left vacant. This decision by the original owners of the bank now allowed Horton to experiment a little with the size of the explosion without worrying too much over the damage it might do to nearby structures.

At precisely 11:30, Horton lit the fuses and made his way back to the horses. He took the bay and the extra horse that he and Joe had brought along in case they were able to capture Delacourte and slowly rode around the edge of town until he came to a concealed position close to Delacourte's house. Delacourte had taken over the empty Finney place on the north edge of town. A large wood frame building standing alone in the center of a city block, it was the closest thing to a mansion in Benton.

As he moved closer to the rear of the house on foot, Horton could see an occasional red glow coming from the back porch, signaling that a guard was enjoying a smoke as he fought boredom and sleep. Horton strained his eyes to find more guards. He finally caught a glimpse of movement at the front of the building. He could find no trace of a third guard, and he doubted that Delacourte would allow anyone to stay inside the house.

Horton checked his watch. He saw that he had ten minutes to wait before midnight. As he snapped the watch closed, a flash of light came from the center of town, followed instantly by the sound of a tremendous explosion. Horton swore silently as lights came on all over town. Something had gone wrong with the fuses at the bank, he knew. He only hoped that Joe had been able to set the charges at the jail before the blast.

In addition to the premature explosion at the bank, another problem became evident. Even before the sound of the blast had stopped echoing through town, both guards on Delacourte's house had gone inside. Horton had hoped that at least one would head into town to investigate the explosion, leaving Delacourte more vulnerable.

Horton sprinted across the open lawn and flattened himself against the side of the house facing away from town. As lights came on in the house, he inched his way to the front corner of the building to await Delacourte's reaction to the blast. He could hear the sounds of shouting coming from town, but so far there was no indication of fire. Horton had not expected fire from the explosions and really did not want one. With the strong wind that was blowing, a fire could level a good portion of the town.

Four minutes after the explosion, Delacourte and the two guards stepped out onto the front porch. Horton, poised with a Colt in each hand, was about to make his play for Delacourte when Brannon and a deputy ran into the yard and up to the porch.

"What was the explosion?" Horton heard Delacourte ask.

"The bank blew up," Brannon answered. "Blew the east side an' the roof in an' pretty much took down the empty store across the street. I left Jasper there to keep folks from pawin' through the wreckage until we can see about the safe."

"I hope the bastard that set it off got caught in the blast," Delacourte said. "He's got to be the dumbest bank robber in history to knock down the whole damned bank."

Brannon and the deputies nodded in agreement. Just then, another, smaller blast came from the center of town, followed soon after by a third from further up the hill.

"Bank robber, hell!" exclaimed Delacourte. "That last one came from over by the jail. We'd better go down and find out what's going on here." The five men started off at a fast walk towards the center of town.

Damn, thought Horton, I'm not getting many breaks tonight. He had known that the possibility of capturing Delacourte tonight was a longshot at best, but now that the opportunity had passed, he found that he was hesitating before taking the next step. He knew that missing Delacourte meant that his element of surprise was gone and that the fight might become a long one.

Horton stuck one of the Colts into his belt and waited a minute or two longer before moving rapidly onto the porch and into the house. He searched the bottom floor quickly and, finding no one, moved up the stairway to the second floor.

"Who's there?" he heard a woman's voice ask from the room to the right of the stairs. "JD, is that you?"

Horton kicked open the door and lunged into the room, pistol ready. He found a woman sitting terror-stricken in the bed. She clutched the blankets around her to cover her nakedness.

Myrna Meloy was, or had been, a strikingly beautiful woman. Now her left eye was blackened, and her upper lip was swollen. Horton caught sight of bruises and what appeared to be bites on her body before she covered herself.

"You'd better get out of here. Jack will kill you if he finds you here," she said, her voice shaking.

"If you're talking about Delacourte, I'm sure he'd try, even if I wasn't in his bedroom. Did I hear you call him Jack?"

"You did. It's short for Jackson. Why do you ask?"

"No special reason. I keep thinking I ought to know that name from somewhere," Horton said thoughtfully. "No matter. What happened to you?" he asked, gesturing towards her bruises.

Myrna blushed. "Jack can't ... he needs to hurt someone ... oh, hell, maybe he just likes to beat people. What business is it of yours?"

"None, ma'am. Now suppose you get dressed and take anything you want to keep with you. You've got about three minutes." Horton took out his watch as if to emphasize the point. He still held the Colt ready in his right hand.

"Three minutes before what? Surely you don't expect me to get dressed with you standing there!" she said indignantly.

"I do, and in three minutes I'm going to burn this house, whether you're dressed or not."

"You're no gentleman, sir! At least you could turn your back!" she exclaimed. "Are you really going to burn the house?"

"I may not be a gentleman, but I won't get shot in the back, either. Now hurry up. You're wasting time."

Myrna sighed in resignation and slid out of bed. Horton found it hard to keep his mind on business. Fortunately for him, Myrna dressed quickly and led the way downstairs. Horton picked up the lamp and followed her.

"There's a can of coal oil on the back porch," she said softly.

Horton looked at her questionably.

"I don't owe JD Delacourte anything. Or maybe I do," she said as she touched her split and swollen lip. "If we're going to burn him out, let's make a good job of it." Before he could stop her, Myrna ducked out the back door and returned almost immediately carrying the can of oil.

Horton holstered his pistol and took the can from Myrna. He went quickly through the bottom floor splashing coal oil on the floors and walls as he went. When he had finished, he opened the front door to help create a draft for the flames and led Myrna to the back of the house. Opening the back door, he turned and hurled the lamp against an inside wall. Instantly the walls and floor erupted into a sea of flame. Horton pulled Myrna through the door and ran with her across the yard into the shadows beyond. Behind them the house blazed fiercely. Once they were safely out of sight, Horton halted.

"Have you got somewhere to go? I doubt that Delacourte will believe that you had nothing to do with this," he said, gesturing towards the burning house.

"I could go back to Fat Ethyl's, I suppose, but he'll just come to get me. I'm wearing everything I own and I'm stone broke. I couldn't get away if I had to."

Horton took her arm and guided her to the spot where the horses were hidden. "I'd planned on using this one for Delacourte tonight. You had better take him instead. If you're smart, you'll head for someplace a long way from here." Horton fished his pockets and produced three double eagles. "You'd better take this," he said, handing coins to the woman. "You'll need it for the trip."

Myrna looked at him, speechless. Finally, she found her voice. "You're General Horton, aren't you? You're the man that the Colonel said he had killed. I'm glad he didn't. Thank you, sir. I'll never be able to repay you for this."

"There's no need to repay me. You helped me tonight and I just returned the favor. Now, I'm going to help you onto the black. When you ride out of here, don't stop for anything until dawn." Horton lifted her onto the horse.

Myrna leaned down and kissed Horton quickly on the cheek. "I was wrong about you. You are a gentleman." She rode off, headed east. She never looked back.

Horton mounted the bay and rode towards the Rafter T. He and Joe had played hell with Delacourte tonight. He wanted to be in position to continue the fight in the morning.

In town, Delacourte and Brannon took inventory of the destruction. The bank and his office were total losses. The jail was heavily damaged, along with the two deputies who were in it. As he was discussing the matter with Brannon, a deputy ran up to them.

"Colonel! Colonel!" he shouted, pointing to the north. "Your house is burning."

A bolt of fear flashed through Delacourte. It was then that he knew for sure that Horton was back. Not only was he back, but he was mad clear through. Delacourte shuddered.

Chapter 12

Dawn found Brannon and Delacourte looking at the smoldering ruins of the latter's house. The structure had been completely destroyed. By the time the town's primitive fire-fighting apparatus had arrived, the entire building had been engulfed in flames. Delacourte was left with only the clothes on his back and a burning hatred in his heart. Horton had struck hard and had made a clean getaway. No one had seen or heard a thing, before or after the attack. If he had not known better, Delacourte would have sworn that he had been hit by a ghost. Or a wolf, he thought, a lobo wolf.

Now that there was some light, the search party Brannon had organized to find Horton would be leaving. Delacourte had little hope that they would find anything. So many people and horses had been milling around the destroyed buildings that finding the tracks of the attacker would be purely accidental. The strong wind that had been blowing all night would help to obscure any tracks Horton might have left, too. Delacourte knew that if he were ever going to catch up with Horton, he must outthink him.

Delacourte motioned for Brannon to join him. "Have you got any ideas how to catch Horton?" he asked.

"I been thinkin' on it, Colonel, an' maybe I do."

"Well, let's hear them. He isn't going to catch himself."

"Maybe he could. You know he was sniffin' around Watkins' daughter pretty good before Ox shot him. I figure that if we get the girl, we get Horton."

"Hmmm," Delacourte said as he considered the idea. "How would you get the word to Horton that we have the girl? We don't know where he is. If we did, we wouldn't need the girl in the first place. We can't just tell the world about it, either. The men in this town would string us up."

"The Watkins girl has been real thick with the Shultz woman over to the cafe lately. I figure we take 'em both an' send the old one after Horton. Tell her that if she tells anyone but Horton, we kill the girl."

Delacourte thought the plan over, trying to see its flaws, but he could find only one: the women might not know where Horton was. If they were to kidnap Watkins' daughter and the Shultz woman and the town were to learn about it, Delacourte knew that everything he had built here would be gone. Texans would stand for a lot of abuse, but not for molesting their women. Rather than discard the plan, however, Delacourte amended it.

"Get the women and take them to the Rafter T. Make sure no one sees you take them. If they don't know where Horton is, we'll have to dispose of them. People may wonder where they've gone, but they won't be able to prove anything. Make sure you take most of their clothes, too. It'll look more like they've gone on a trip."

"Right, Colonel. When is it you want I should git 'em?"

"A couple of hours after dark should be about right. There will be fewer people around to ask questions. I'll take two of the boys and go out to the ranch now."

"But boss, I only got four men left as it is," Brannon complained, "an' two of them're out lookin' for Horton's tracks."

"Now you have only the two looking for Horton. Get some more men. With Horton on the loose, neither of us should be out alone. He could be anywhere."

"Why not stay at the hotel, Colonel? We could keep an eye on it and still run everything else."

"Like you kept an eye on the office and bank? Hell, Brannon, you couldn't even guard the jail! I'm going out to the ranch, where at least I can see him coming. You come out when you get the women. Once we get Horton, we can take back the town. Nothing has really changed here."

"When you get to the ranch, can you send the men back? The boys already there ought to be able to take care of Horton if he shows up."

"Those men are just cowmen. I doubt that they could handle someone like Horton. I'm not very sure of your deputies, for that matter. No, you'll have to make do with those two who are out looking for tracks. If they do their usual job, they'll be back before noon, empty handed."

Brannon cussed as he stomped off to get the deputies for Delacourte. This whole operation was going sour as far as he was concerned. He also was convinced that more than buildings had been destroyed last night. The town had seen that someone could hurt Delacourte without being hurt in return. He was no longer invincible. Brannon also thought that Delacourte had lost his guts. He began to make plans for getting rid of the colonel just as soon as Horton was killed. Maybe, he mused, I could even make it look like they finished off each other. With that happy thought, he turned his attention to the problem of capturing the women.

Horton and Joe lay quietly in their concealed position on the crest of a long hill a quarter mile south of the Rafter T headquarters. They had watched Delacourte and two deputies ride in an hour earlier. Several men had ridden out some time later, but none had taken the road to Benton. Neither of the two deputies had been with them.

Both Horton and Joe thought that the riders were part of the crew that ran the ranch. They were tough men, mostly veterans of the rebellion and all seasoned by the dangers of the frontier. They were, however, mostly honest men who worked hard for a fair wage. They were not gunmen, but they would fight fiercely if called upon to defend themselves. Whether they would take sides in this fight between himself and Delacourte was still not known. Horton thought that few would side with Delacourte. He also recognized that none would side with him. The plan he and Joe had worked out called for avoiding these riders whenever possible.

After the riders were out of sight, Joe gathered up his Sharps and ammunition. "I'll be goin' now, boss. I'll hit the north line camp first, then swing on east an' get that one, too. After that, I'll take up my position on that hill yonder," he said, pointing to a hill overlooking the road leading from town to the Rafter T. "I can cover the front of the house good from there an' you can cover the back of the house an' the bunkhouse from here."

"I'm going to move west about two hundred yards after you get back," Horton answered. "It'll give me a better field of fire on the back of the house, but I won't be able to cover the road. You'll have to do that. Be sure you swing by here when you get back. Take care that you don't get lost out there all by yourself."

"I been carin' for me a durn site longer than I care to remind myself. An' why all the sudden concern, anyway? 'Peers to me you weren't too concerned last night, what you startin' the war early an' all. Someday I'm goin' to set you down an' learn you either how to cut fuse or tell time, or maybe even both. Come to think on it, I doubt you could learn two things at once." Joe smiled at Horton. "Only thing bothers me is leavin' you here alone while I'm gone. Wished I'd of brought along a wet nurse to look after you."

Horton laughed. "Take care of yourself, old man. Nasty as you are, I believe I'd still miss you. You'd better leave if you're going to make it back tonight."

Joe walked back to where the horses were hidden. A few minutes later, Horton heard Joe ride off. His position was well-suited for keeping the house under observation. Delacourte was accounted for, but he did not want to assault the house until he knew where Brannon was. Brannon, he knew, was the most dangerous of the men he would have to face. Horton settled in for a long wait. Brannon would be coming sooner or later. When he did, Horton would be ready.

Joe bellied up behind a little rise in front of the Rafter T's northern line camp just before noon. Cupping his hands to his mouth, he hollered a "Hello" at the cabin. The door opened and two men walked out. One of them carried a Spencer in his hands.

"Hold it, boys. I just want to talk for a minute," Joe said.

"I don't talk to people I can't see," the man with the Spencer said. "Come on in an' we'll talk a spell."

"I'm goin' to stay right here, boys, if'n you don't mind. I'm Joe Penbrook from over to the Circle H. Me an' my boss got us a shootin' war with your boss. I come here today to burn this place out an' I just as soon not have anyone get shot up while I'm doin' it."

The two men at the door exchanged glances. The man with the rifle spoke again. "We don't want no part of your war, but we got all our stuff inside and month's wages due. Reckon we'd have to fight to keep what's ours."

"Take your time movin' out, boys. I'll pay your back wages if that's all that's keepin' you. When you leave, you can ride over to the Circle H an' wait for us if you want another ridin' job. May take us a few days to get there, though."

The men discussed the matter briefly and then the one without the rifle walked slowly back inside. The other man said, "We'll be goin', Mister Penbrook. We'll even wait a couple of days at the Circle H. If we get tired of waitin' we'll just move on." The other man emerged from the cabin and dragged his gear out into the yard.

Joe stood up and moved into the yard. He walked up to the two men and gave them each forty dollars. "The extra ten is to work a week at Circle H cleanin' up the place best you can. Delacourte tried to burn it down but didn't quite finish it. I'd like one of you boys to go back to the Rafter T an' tell the rest of 'em there the same thing I told you. Horton an' me'll think that anybody there after dark tonight is sidin' with Delacourte an' buying into this here war."

The men pocketed the money. "Would you really have shot us if we'd stayed?" the rifleman asked.

"Guess we'll never know for sure, will we?" Joe responded. The three men smiled at each other.

Along about mid-afternoon, Horton saw a rider approach the Rafter T from the north. He rode directly to the bunkhouse, dismounted and went in. Twenty minutes later, a half-dozen men emerged carrying their gear and walked to the corral. They caught up their horses, saddled up and rode northeast away from the ranch. The first rider emerged from the bunkhouse with a sack a few moments later, remounted his horse and turned to face the hill from which Horton was watching. The man flipped a salute towards the hill and rode off after the others.

"I wonder what that was all about?" Horton said under his breath as he went back to watching the house.

Max Brannon pulled a dirty handkerchief from his pocket and polished the star on his chest. He belched loudly and pushed himself away from the table. As he stood, he pocketed the handkerchief and checked his watch. "Eight o'clock. Time to go," he said to Carp Applegate, one of the two deputies Delacourte had left him. The other deputy, Jasper Brown, was at the livery getting the horses ready for the ride to the ranch.

Brannon had hired two more deputies that morning. They were rough men; gunmen used to hardship and without scruples. Brannon was glad to have them. All three were to meet Max and Carp at the Watkins house.

Carp nodded and put on his hat. He was a tall, thin man with a face so narrow that his eyes nearly touched. He had a habit of opening and closing his mouth frequently, like a fish stranded on the shore. It was from this habit that he got his name. He was a mean man who enjoyed inflicting pain on others. He and Max had been together since before the war, and Max had found him to be a master at extracting information from men who were reluctant to talk. Tonight, Max had said that he would have a chance to work on some women. Carp worked his mouth rapidly in anticipation. This would be a first for him, if he didn't count a whore or two at Fat Ethyl's, and he was anxious to get started.

Max and Carp walked out of the hotel and stood on the porch for a few moments as they checked the street. The front windows of the hotel were boarded up as a result of the blast at the bank diagonally across the street. The two men crossed to the bank and headed up the street towards Marta's house. There was little activity on the street, and that pleased Max. He did not want any witnesses to what they were about to do.

They found Marta's house deserted when they got there. Max broke a window and boosted Carp inside. Carp checked the house and found Marta's wardrobe empty. On the way out, he spotted a pie on the kitchen table. He took it with him as he went, lifting chunks of it out of the dish with his fingers. "Want some?" he asked, offering the dish to Max.

"Get rid of that stuff," Brannon said gruffly. "We ain't got time for that." He cuffed the dish from Carp's hands.

"Now what'd you do that for?" Carp whined, licking his sticky fingers and then wiping them on his pants. "You got no call to do that."

"You damn fool, just try drawin' a gun with your hand full of pie. Sometimes I don't think you got a brain in your head." Brannon gave Carp a shove towards the Watkins house. "Now get walkin' and keep your eyes open." Muttering under his breath, Carp started up the street.

The Watkins house was on the opposite side of the street from Marta's. Max and Carp walked past the house before crossing the street. As they walked past, they could see Sarah sitting alone in the parlor, reading.

Once across the street, Max sent Carp around to the rear of the house while he mounted the front steps and knocked softly on the door.

He heard footsteps approaching the door and Sarah's voice ask, "Who is it?"

"It's me, Seth Horton," answered Max. He smiled slyly as the door opened slowly.

"Come in, Seth," he heard Sarah say coyly.

Max pushed the door open and found Sarah standing well back from the door, hands behind her back.

"Why, it's Sheriff Brannon! Why ever did you say that you were Seth Horton?" she asked sweetly.

Max closed the door behind him and leaned back against it. He let his eyes roam freely over her full figure. He licked his lips and vowed, not for the first time, that someday he'd take this wench. Reluctantly, he brought his eyes back to her face and said, "Thought you might let him in quicker 'n you let me in. Suppose me an' you go for a little ride. The colonel wanted to see you." Smiling, he reached out a hand to take her arm.

In one smooth motion, Sarah brought a Colt Navy out from behind her back and, steadying her right hand with her left, fired. The bottom half inch of Max's left ear vanished in a small spray of blood. His smile vanished with it.

Max yelped and clasped his left hand to his roached ear. He thought of killing her then, but the sight of the cocked pistol pointing directly at his face effectively discouraged the idea. His eyes watering from the pain of his ear and the particles of black powder that had burned his face, Max waited patiently for Carp to come in through the back door. The sound of a pistol shot followed quickly by Carp's scream told him that he could expect no further help from that quarter.

"I got him," he heard Marta say. "I think I killed him."

For the first time, Brannon was really worried.

"Brannon, you murdering bastard, what gave you the idea I'd go anywhere with you?" Sarah spat. "You're very close to dying right here, right now." Her manner left no doubt in his mind that she was absolutely serious.

"Now, ma'am, don't do nuthin' hasty," he said, raising his right hand as if to ward off another shot "I ain't never done nuthin' to you."

"Not to my father, either, I suppose." Sarah fired again, and the ring finger on his right hand dangled by a thread of skin. Max screamed and grasped his battered right hand with his left. "Don't ... don't shoot me no more," he pleaded.

"Is that what my father said?" She fired again and watched blood well out of the hole that appeared in the toe of his left boot. Max groaned and fell back against the door, then sank to the floor.

"Hear me, Brannon. I've got three shots left in this pistol and another Colt ready when this one is empty. If you want to live through the night, you'd better do exactly what I tell you."

"Anything you say, ma'am," he said. "Anything at all. Just don't shoot me no more."

"First, take off that badge. You disgrace it."

He snatched the badge from his chest and flung it from him as if it were red hot.

"Now take out your pistol with two fingers and toss it over here."

Brannon complied.

"I want you to go tell Delacourte for me that he's a dead man. The next time I see him, I'll kill him, wherever he is. If anyone lifts a hand towards me after tonight, this town will tear him apart, and you know it. You've lost, Brannon, you and Delacourte both. Get out of here before I change my mind and kill you right now. Just give me an excuse to do it. Please."

Brannon was shaken. He pulled himself to his feet and started to open the door.

"Three men coming up behind the house," Marta shouted.

"You'd better get out there and stop them, Brannon. You're running out of time and I'm running out of patience."

Brannon flung himself through the door and, limping badly, made his way towards the horsemen coming up to the back of the house. Looking through a window, he could see the outline of Sarah, who now had what looked like a Henry in her hands. He knew that she would know how to use it.

"Jasper! You other men! Stay where you are!" Max shouted.

"And take that thing with you," he heard Marta say.

Max detoured to the back porch and, grabbing a handful of Carp's shirt, dragged the body towards the horsemen.

"Give me a hand with him," he gasped as he neared the group. Jasper and one of the new men dismounted and put the body on one of the horses that had been intended for the women.

"What'll we do now, boss?" Jasper asked.

"First thing we're goin' to do is see Doc Waterman. Then we'll get us a drink and go out to the Rafter T. If the colonel wants those damn spitfires, he can damn well come in an' get 'em himself. He don't pay me enough money to go back in there." Max paused to catch his breath, then looked at Jasper and said, "Give me your extra gun."

Jasper drew a Dance Brothers pistol from his belt and passed it to Brannon. Max thrust the pistol into his empty holster.

One of the new men laughed. The sound died quickly under Brannon's icy stare. "We've stood here long enough," Brannon said as he mounted. "Let's go." The men rode out onto the street and headed for Doc Waterman's place.

Inside the house, the two women sat down with obvious relief at the kitchen table. Sarah got back up and brought a small wooden box back to the table. She opened the box, revealing a small can of oil, some rags, and a short cleaning rod. Slowly she began to disassemble the Colt for cleaning.

"Why didn't you kill Brannon while you had the chance?" Marta asked.

"I wanted to hurt him a little and make him sweat at first. After the second shot, I realized that if I killed him, I would be no better than he was. At the end, I knew that I needed him to stop the other three coming up at the back of the house." Sarah paused as she ran an oily cloth through the barrel of the pistol. "I guess I'm glad that I didn't kill him. Every time he looks at that right hand or changes his socks, he'll be reminded that he got whipped by a woman."

"He probably doesn't ever change his socks. I still think you should have finished him off while you had the chance. Now somebody else is going to have to do it."

"That's fine with me, Marta. I don't need any more revenge. I don't like what it does to me," Sarah said as she reassembled the pistol. She reloaded the empty chambers and laid the pistol on the table. "Now just let 'em come back. I'm ready."

Marta laughed as she reached for the box so that she could clean and reload her pistol.

The three Horton brothers were sitting at a table in Delacourte's saloon. They had made the ride from Pueblo to Benton in eight days by changing horses frequently and riding far into the night. They knew from talking with Fred Handlemann in Pueblo what the general situation was between the Circle H and Delacourte. They had stopped in town to get a drink and to see Ira Watkins before riding out to the Circle H.

By listening to the barroom chatter for the past hour or so, they had learned of Seth's attack on Delacourte's strongholds and of Ira Watkins' murder. The brothers were discussing what their next move should be when Brannon limped through the batwing doors with his two deputies. Brannon grabbed the bottle offered by the bartender and made his way to a table near the back door. The deputies followed him at a distance. Once seated, they conversed in low tones among themselves, rapidly lowering the level of whiskey in the bottle as they talked. From time to time, Brannon or one of the other men would look over at the Hortons and then resume their discussion. After a few minutes, Brannon and his group got up and walked towards the Hortons' table, leaving an empty bottle on the table behind them.

Brannon's crew pulled to a stop in front of the Hortons, who slowly got to their feet, expecting trouble.

"Don't get up, boys. We seen you sittin' there an' thought we'd come over an' say howdy. You're strangers around here, ain't you?" Brannon inquired.

Marcus said, "No stranger than anyone else in this pig pen, I reckon."

Brannon smiled. "Yeah, it ain't much, is it?" It was a statement of fact, not a question. He looked the men over slowly and said, "You boys wouldn't be lookin' for jobs, would you?"

"Might be," Marcus said, "dependin' on what the job was to be."

"I need some more deputies who know how to use their guns. I make you boys out as knowin' how it's done. What do you say?"

"Well, we ain't much used to working with the law," Marcus responded. "We might not know just how to act."

Brannon laughed this time. "Thought so," he said. "To tell you the truth, there ain't a whole lot of law work connected with the job." Brannon surveyed the remnants of the Confederate uniforms that the men wore. "What I'm goin' to do is run out a Yankee named Horton, if I don't bury him first."

"Is that how you got that?" Marcus asked, pointing to Brannon's right hand. Three fingers and a thumb protruded from the bloody bandage that covered most of the hand. "That ear don't look none too healthy, either."

The deputies laughed and Brannon's face and neck flamed. "The daughter of the former sheriff done this from ambush. When this Horton fellow is done for, we'll come back for her, her and that Shultz bitch."

Matthew spoke up. "Marcus, I don't know if I want to be part of an outfit that gets run off by just one man and a girl. We might be better off doin' the job alone without the handicap of havin' these fellers along. Ask him who the real boss is. We'll talk to him."

Brannon turned ugly. "You got three choices, loudmouth. You work for me, you leave town, or you die. What'll it be?"

Marcus smiled coldly and said, "There's a fourth choice. We could work for the Circle H, I'll bet."

"What are you," Brannon asked sarcastically, "friends of this guy Horton?"

"Nope," answered Marcus. "We're his brothers."

A moment of silence descended over the saloon followed quickly by the roaring of six-guns. In a matter of seconds, the room was filled with the gray smoke of burning black powder. Brannon and Cal Zimmer, one of the new deputies, ran through the back of the saloon and into the alley, taking fragments of the back door with them as they went.

"Let's get the hell out of here!" cried Brannon. He got no argument from Zimmer.

Inside, Marcus surveyed the battlefield as the smoke lifted. Two deputies were shot to rags, either dead or so close to it that it no longer mattered. James had taken a slug high up in the left part of his chest, but since he wasn't foaming blood from the wound or his mouth, it was unlikely that the lung had been touched. Marcus had been bullet-notched along his right side and left leg, but he wouldn't label either as a real wound. Matthew appeared to be untouched. Slowly the other patrons of the saloon got up off the floor as the Hortons reloaded their pistols. The place was filled with the buzz of conversation.

Matthew was the first to speak. "Well, Marcus, what'll we do now?" he asked.

"First off, we better git Jim here to Doc Waterman's. Then I suggest we go see Sarah Watkins. She had some reason for shootin' Brannon, an' I'll bet it had a lot to do with Seth. I need to talk to you boys a little first, though," he added. "The three of us here was blazin' away with four or five shots apiece an' all we got was half the targets. Gawd, it's no wonder we lost the war. The Yanks must have learned how to spread their fire. Next time maybe I'll just stand aside and pick off the ones y'all leave standin'.'" Fortunately for Marcus, he was smiling as he talked.

"Yes, Captain. We done heard that lecture before," said Matthew.

"Yeah, like maybe a million times," added Jim. "Let's go to Doc's before I bleed to death or die of old age." The men holstered their weapons and walked out of the saloon.

The Hortons found Doc Waterman putting on his coat.

"Well, I'll be durned," he said. "The last of the Hortons accounted for. Did you boys have something to do with shooting up Brannon an hour or so ago?"

"No," Marcus answered, "I understand that Sarah Watkins did that. We just got done with Brannon's bunch over to Delacourte's saloon."

"Good for Sarah!" Doc exclaimed. Then he added more softly, "Any reason for me to go over to the saloon?"

"Only if you want a drink, Doc," Jim said. "The two hombres we left there don't need your help. The two that run away was goin' too fast to be bad hurt. I'd 'preciate it if you'd fix me up a mite before you go for that drink, though." Jim walked carefully to the examination table and laid down.

The doctor looked at Jim's wound and then at Marcus' notches. He sent Matthew to help clean and bandage Marcus while he poked around for the slug still in Jim's chest. He extracted the .36 caliber ball deftly and handed it to Jim.

"Here, son," he said. "You might want to keep this for a souvenir. Three inches to the right and a little lower and you wouldn't have had to worry about it."

Jim sat up and examined the ball, then slipped it into his pocket. He laid back down again, looking very pale.

Doc walked over to Marcus, who was pulling his shirt over a bandage on his side. "Your brother will be just fine, but I think he ought to stay here tonight. If you don't leave him here, you definitely must keep him quiet. Riding is, of course, out of the question for at least a week."

"Alright, Doc, we'll leave him here for tonight and thank you for your kindness. One of us will be back for him in the mornin'."

"I'm a real kind fellow alright, but that doesn't mean I work for free. That'll be three dollars for the patchin'. There'll be no charge for the bed tonight." Doc extended his hand in anticipation of payment.

Marcus handed Doc a dollar. "Jim got the most patchin'. You'd better collect the rest from him."

Jim raised himself up on one elbow and spoke weakly. "Marcus, give the man his money. You give the word 'cheap' a whole new meanin'."

Grumbling good-naturedly, Marcus forked over the other two dollars. After he put on his hat, he turned to Jim and said, "Rest easy tonight, Jim. We'll get you tomorrow. For now, you'd better get some rest." Jim nodded in agreement and lowered himself back on the table.

Matt and Marcus left Doc Waterman's place and walked up the street towards the Watkins house. When they reached it, Marcus cupped his hands to his mouth and yelled, "Hello, the house!"

"Hello, yourself. What do you want?" came the response.

"Just some talk. Can we come up?"

"Who are you?" Sarah responded.

"Matt and Marcus Horton," came the reply.

The door opened and Sarah came out on the porch, a Colt pistol clutched in her hand. "Just don't stand there hollering in the street. Come on up. You're disturbin' the neighbors."

When the two men walked up onto the porch, Sarah walked up and hugged them both. "Welcome home, boys. You got here just in time. Come on into the house where I can see you better." Turning towards the door, Sarah said, "I'm coming in, Marta. You can put up the shotgun." The two men followed Sarah into the house.

It took more than an hour for the two women to bring the Horton brothers up to date on what had been happening since Delacourte had arrived in town. They followed with interest the story of Seth's shootout at Jenkins' saloon and the subsequent raid on Delacourte's strongholds in town.

"'Peers like we missed out on most of the fun, brother," Matt said. "That Yankee brother of ours seems to have Delacourte on the run. We better get out to the Rafter T before the war ends without us."

"I think you had better wait until morning before you start wandering around the Rafter T looking for Seth," Sarah advised. "He doesn't know you're back and he isn't expecting any other help. He and Joe might just shoot anyone they caught moving up on them."

"Good advice, Sarah. We'll time it so's we get there after sunup," Marcus offered. "We'd appreciate it if you or Marta would go to Doc Waterman's in the mornin' an' pick up Jim. Maybe he could stay with y'all until we get back."

"We'll both go," said Marta. "I don't think anyone will make another try for us, but Sarah and I decided that we'll do everything together until this matter is settled once and for all."

"Then it's settled. If you don't mind us beddin' down in your parlor, Matt an' me will keep guard tonight while you ladies get some sleep. You've had a real full day, it seems to me. We'll start out to Rafter T about an hour before dawn. It'll be plenty light by the time we get there."

"Of course you can stay here," Sarah answered, "but Marta and I will take our turns watching, too." Marta nodded in agreement. "You men go on and get some sleep. You can use father's room at the head of the stairs. When you're on watch, Marta and I double up. Now get going. I think that you're the ones who are going to have a full day tomorrow."

A few minutes later Sarah heard the gentle sounds of snoring coming from upstairs. She found herself wondering if Seth snored, too, and then became a little embarrassed by the implications of her thoughts. She turned the lamp very low and settled into her vantage point by the window next to the front door. "Please, God, let it be quiet tonight," she prayed silently.

Somewhere in town, a dog barked frantically and then stopped with a yelp. The night stayed quiet except for the soft whispering of the wind.

It was not a quiet night everywhere. When Max Brannon and Cal Zimmer ran from the saloon, they went directly to the livery. Brannon saddled his horse, a large buckskin, while Cal threw his rig on the first horse he came across, a mean-looking, roman-nosed chestnut. They mounted and rode as fast as they could for the Rafter T. All the way to the ranch, Max thought about what he would tell Delacourte. He was no longer making plans for forcing Delacourte out of the picture. Brannon's confidence had gone the way of his badge and his missing finger. He was a beaten man, desperate for guidance. He finally decided to tell Delacourte as much of the truth as he could until the colonel started showing signs of rage, then shut up and take his chances. It wasn't a good plan, he knew, but it was the best he could come up with at the moment.

From the hill overlooking the Rafter T, Joe Penbrook heard the sound of approaching riders. He shifted his position so that he could better observe the road. The riders were nearly abreast of him before he recognized Max Brannon's horse. By the time he had retrieved the big Sharps and had drawn a bead on Brannon, the horsemen had covered more than a hundred yards. Joe aligned his sights on the middle of the lighter of the two masses and squeezed the trigger.

The sound of the shot echoed through the valley. Max heard the crash of the rifle and felt the big buckskin hesitate in mid-stride. The next thing he knew, he was being catapulted over his dead horse's head.

He struck the ground hard, driving the breath from his lungs. Dazed and shaken, Brannon fought to catch his breath. He was reasonably certain that every bone in his body was broken. Somewhat to his surprise, he found that he could get to his feet. He had staggered a dozen or more steps towards the ranch house by the time Cal managed to stop his horse and return for him. Max doubted that he would have returned the favor for Cal if the roles had been reversed, but that did not stop him from accepting the stirrup and assisting hand that were offered so that he could swing up behind Cal. The men reached the house without further mishap.

Dismounting quickly in front of the house, both men dashed for the door. When they entered the house, they found themselves looking into the bores of a half-dozen pistols held by Delacourte and his men. Delacourte holstered his pistol when he recognized Brannon.

"You took your own sweet time getting here, Brannon. Where are the women? What was that shot out there a minute ago?"

"It's kind of a long story, Colonel. Can we go somewhere and talk, private-like?"

Delacourte turned to the men behind him and nodded towards an open doorway.

"You other men clear out of here for a while." As soon as the room was cleared, he turned back to Brannon.

"What happened to you? You look like you got caught in a stampede. Where's your badge?"

"I lost it," Max mumbled in reply.

"Where are the women? I told you to bring them here tonight," Delacourte demanded.

Brannon related the story to Delacourte as best he could. Delacourte's expression changed from one of disgust to that of astonishment, and finally to one of anger.

"You mean to hell me that two women ran off five heavily armed men, all of whom were officers of the law? That's impossible!" Delacourte exploded.

"Well, they got the drop on us," Brannon explained miserably.

"Then what happened?"

"We went to Doc Waterman's. He finished cuttin' off my finger an' took care of my foot. Then we dropped Carp's body off to get planted. After that, we all went to the saloon to get a drink before we tried again for the women," Max lied.

"Is that where the other men are? In my saloon, drunk?"

"They're in the saloon, alright, but they ain't drunk. Last I saw, they was deader 'n hell."

"Dead? I can't believe it! Every time you go somewhere, you manage to get more of my men killed off. How did you manage it this time?"

Max looked away from Delacourte in embarrassment. "We run across the Hortons."

"You ran across Horton in my saloon and the four of you couldn't kill him? You idiots!" Delacourte raged.

"I didn't say I ran across this Horton. I ran across three more of 'em. The other brothers finally made it back home from the war."

"That's even worse! Now I've got four Hortons to worry about. Is that how your other two deputies got themselves killed? Did you manage to get any of them, or would that be asking too much from you?" Delacourte shouted.

"I think we might have got some lead into one of 'em." Brannon paused for a moment, then added softly, "Maybe."

"You incompetent fool! How could you let such a thing happen?"

"They got the drop on us, boss," Max said humbly.

"You stupid bastard, everybody in the state of Texas has had the drop on you!" With that, Delacourte drew his pistol and shot Brannon as fast as he could, repeatedly cocking the hammer and pulling the trigger until the pistol was empty. It all happened so quickly that the look of shocked surprise was frozen on Brannon's face as he was slammed back against the wall by the impact of the slugs. He crumbled slowly to the floor, dead.

Cal and the other men crowded back into the smoky room.

"What happened, Colonel?" Cal asked.

"He crossed me, that's what happened. Now drag his body outside and set up a watch. "You," he said, pointing to Cal, "What's your name?"

I'm Cal Zimmer, sir."

"Well, you're in charge now. Get the watch set. In the morning we'll work out a plan for getting rid of the Hortons once and for all."

"Yes, sir. I'll get on it right away."

"Just don't be like Brannon. If you turn out to be as stupid as he was, you won't last long, either."

"I plan on bein' around for a long time, Colonel."

"So do I," Delacourte responded, "so do I."

Chapter 13

Marcus and Matt were awakened by the sounds and smells of cooking coming from the kitchen. Mat struck a match and lit the lamp on the bed stand.

"Gawd, Matthew, you sure could do with a bath," Marcus sniffed as the two men competed for the first use of the basin and pitcher on the washstand.

"You ain't no bed of roses yourself, big brother. I don't reckon we'll get a chance to today, but when this whole thing's over, I'm goin' to soak in a tub of hot water for a week an' then sleep for a month. That's right after I eat a steer, hair and all."

"It's nice to see a young man with a goal in life," Marcus responded as he wiped the water from his face and hands. "Me, I'd settle for a shave. If you'll hurry, we can go downstairs an' see what the ladies have been up to. Nobody woke me to stand watch last night."

"Me neither," Matt said. "Too late to worry about it now, but I hope they didn't just fall asleep down there an' leave no one watchin'. It scares me a little just thinkin' about that possibility."

"Know what you mean," Marcus said as he stomped on his boots over his bare feet. Neither man had even seen a sock for three years or more, and neither considered them to be necessities any longer. "I expect that those women decided to give us some slack an' take turns standin' watch without us."

"To tell you the truth, brother, I wouldn't want to try sneakin' up on either one of 'em. Judgin' by what happened yesterday, I'd say that they both knew how to handle a gun and that neither of 'em are a bit shy about usin' 'em either. They'll both do to take along. You ready to go down yet?"

Marcus nodded that he was ready and the men made their way downstairs, carrying the lamp with them. It was still pitch-black outside, and Marcus wondered idly what time it was. He had lost his silver hunter-cased watch shortly after Gettysburg by thinking that the three jacks he held were going to win a pot. A full house in the hand of his company commander had kept him guessing about the time ever since.

When the men reached the kitchen, they found a breakfast of eggs, hot cakes, side meat, and coffee waiting for them. After exchanging "good mornings," they all sat down to eat. There was little talk at the table as the men set about the business of eating. It did not take long for the food to disappear. When they all had eaten their fill, Marcus pushed his chair back from the table and cleared his throat.

"Mighty fine breakfast, ladies. I haven't eaten that well since before the war, an' that ain't no lie. I didn't hardly recognize what real coffee tasted like without burnt bread and chicory stuck into it. Thinkin' back, I don't know why we didn't come home as soon as the war was over. Seems to me that we had a reason at the time, but whatever it was, it can't compare to this breakfast."

"They say that in old age the memory is the second thing to go, big brother. I can still remember the reason. We stayed away so long so we could make our fortune in the gold fields. We're dressed so elegant," Matt continued, dusting off his much-patched butternut uniform jacket, "because we was so successful at it, too. Still, we done better than most. We nearly broke even."

The women laughed. Sarah said, "Well, I'm still glad you high rollers are back. I know Seth will be greatly relieved, too. He's sent wires all over the country asking about you all." She paused for a moment, then continued. "It may not be my place to say it, but I think that Seth feels a little guilty sometimes for not having resigned his commission and come home when the war started. It's not because he thinks the Confederacy was right, mind you. I believe it's more because he thinks his decision might have driven a wedge between you brothers."

"He needn't worry none on that score," Marcus responded. "We was all raised around our place to be independent thinkers an' to do what we thought best. We all did an' Enoch paid the full price for his beliefs. The rest of us got off pretty light, considerin' everything. I think it's a new day now, an' we'd all be well-served to put what's past behind us. Blood counts for more than different opinions, anyhow." His eyes began to twinkle. "You can rest easy on another score, too. We ain't shot a Yankee in more 'n a year. If you an' Seth wasn't so thick, I'd be real tempted, though, just to cut down on the competition."

Sarah blushed furiously and the rest laughed at her discomfort. "Go ahead and have a good laugh while you can. The country is crawling with us old widow women all looking for flirty men who make rash statements and can't run too fast. We all shoot pretty good, too, so don't be getting any ideas about doing us wrong. We've been known to get even." Marta nodded her head in agreement and joined Sarah in laughter. The men pretended to look repentant.

"Much as I hate to break up this happy group, I think we'd better get started for the Rafter T. You about ready to go, Matt?"

Matt answered by getting up from the table and buckling on his gun belt. "If you're waitin' on me, you're already late, brother. Let's go."

Sarah hugged each of them. "Don't worry about Jim. He'll be here when you get back. Take care of yourselves and bring Seth and Joe back all in one piece." She handed Marcus her Henry and a box of shells. "You may need this before it's all over. Take care."

The men assured her they would and Marcus thanked her for the rifle. "I always wanted one of these Yankee rifles you could load on a Sunday and shoot all week. You can bet that I'll take good care of it." Both men made their way out of the house and down the street to the livery. Ten minutes later they were riding out of town towards the Rafter T.

Joe Penbrook was deciding what to do about breakfast. The sun had been up for more than an hour and so far he had seen nothing move in the ranch yard. He decided that he could eat some cold biscuits and beans. It was the decision about building a fire to make coffee that bothered him. As badly as he wanted coffee, he still didn't want to give away his exact position unnecessarily. Finally, he moved about fifty yards and built a small fire. He used the last of the water from his canteen to make the coffee.

"That coffee sure smells good, Joe. Got enough for us?" Joe whirled quickly and pawed for the pistol on his hip. He knew that he was a dead man. Damn, he thought in an instant, I never thought I'd die 'cause of a cup of coffee.

"Whoa there, Joe. It's only us, Matt and Marcus." As usual, it was Marcus doing the talking. "We came out here to give you a hand, not watch a fast draw demonstration. Now look what you've done. You spilled the coffee. Got any more beans?"

"Yeah, but I'm out of water. Now I know how Seth felt at Beckley's store the other night," Joe said, holstering his pistol. He noted that his hands were shaking.

"How's that?" Joe asked.

"Never mind. It's a private story. When did you two pups get back? Where's James? Have you been to town yet? How did you know we was here? Where ...."

"Now hold on there, Joe. We'll answer all your questions, but one at a time. Matt, will you get your canteen? This ol' buzzard's probably all dried out from askin' so many questions."

"If'n you weren't so wet behind the ears, I'd dry you two out pronto for sneakin' up behind a man. Ain't you two got no manners?" Joe asked indignantly.

"We're glad to see you, too, Joe. Where's Seth?"

"He's across the road on the other hill, coverin' the back of the place."

"What's the plan?"

"Tell you when Matt gets back so I don't have to do it twice." Joe looked at the Henry in Marcus' hands. "Where'd you get that?"

"Sarah gave it to me when we left this mornin'. 'Bout didn't make it. She 'n Marta Shultz fed us 'til we was about to bust. Was I an old man like you, I'd latch onto that Marta. She can cook like no one I ever seen."

"If she brought out some hotcakes and coffee, I believe I would. Now that you boys are done tryin' to scare me to death, I could do a good job eatin' a bear, fur an' all."

Matt came back to the fire and tossed the canteen to Joe. "There's the water, Joe. I brung you some bacon I snitched at breakfast this mornin'. Ain't much, but it beats nothin'."

"'Preciate that, Matt. Almost makes up for you causin' my heart to stop beatin'. Now supposin' you two set a spell an' tell me what I ought to know, that is, if it ain't askin' too much."

For the next ten minutes the men filled each other in on what had taken place, both in town and at the ranch. When the Hortons got finished with the story of the shootout at Sarah's, Joe clapped his hands and let out a whoop.

"Good for them women!" he exclaimed. "Seth was some worried that Delacourte's bunch might try somethin' like that, but he couldn't talk them hard-headed girls into leavin' town. He an' Sarah both got real tight jawed, but she got her way. Seems like she was right, too."

"That Sarah is quite a woman. Seth's lucky to have her," Marcus observed.

"He is that, but I ain't all that sure that he knows he's got her. For that matter, I ain't positive that he wants her, although I seen some signs that point in that direction."

"If he's too dumb to latch on to her, you can be sure I'm goin' to be first in line to start courtin'. Man don't find a woman like that ever' day."

"You might just have to fight with me," Matt said. "I kind of favor her, too."

"She's a fine girl, alright, but a might skinny for me. I'd rather they had a bit more meat on their bones, like Marta. Now, there's a woman!" As far as Joe was concerned, the conversation was over.

It was just a well, for at that moment Matt pointed and said, "Look! There's a man runnin' from the house to the barn."

A second or two later a crash from the opposite hill announced that Seth had seen the man, too, and had gotten off a shot. The running man was flung sideways six or eight feet, where he collapsed into a heap. Even at this range anyone could tell that the man was dead.

"Gawd, what kind of cannon is Seth usin', anyway?" Matt asked in wonder.

"Sharps .50, same as me," Joe answered.

"Why? He ain't figurin' on huntin' trains, is he?"

"Seth likes the range and accuracy. He wants to pick 'em off for a while an' then get Delacourte when the odds is better an' they're real jumpy. He'll probably want to try somethin' tonight, when we can sneak in close."

"Hell, let's ride in there now. We got enough men to do the job," Matt suggested.

"If we do, some of us is likely to get hurt, permanent. Seth talked like he wanted to walk away after this one was over," Joe replied.

"I think Seth's probably right. There ain't no hurry, so there ain't no real sense in makin' a charge. How many folks are in that place, anyway, Joe?" Marcus asked.

"I make it about a half dozen. Delacourte rode in with two deputies. Brannon brought one with him, an' I figure two, maybe three of the ranch hands stayed to fight for the brand. That lump out on the front porch is Brannon, an' Seth just fetched another that I don't recognize, so that leaves five or six, way I count."

"Sure glad there ain't more than ten," Matthew said. "If there was, you'd probably have to take off your boots to count higher 'n that."

"You damn boys is all the same—sassy, clean through. Got no respect for age, brains, or your betters. Were I a bit younger, I'd put you over my knee an' teach you how to count," Joe growled.

"Wouldn't be no use, Joe," Marcus said. "Didn't work when you tried it years ago an' won't work now. You'll have to try somethin' else."

"I give up on the both of you. Why don't you go over an' pester your other brother. Maybe I'll get lucky an' he'll shoot you."

"Believe we will. I got a fair fix on his smoke when he fired," Marcus said.

"Then you better look twenty, thirty yards one way or t'other. He don't stay put worth a damn after he's marked his position," Joe volunteered.

"Thanks. We heard a lot about ol' Wolf, or Lobo as our boys called him when they was mad at him, which was most of the time. They said he was a mean, dangerous man. That talk caused us a lot of trouble from time to time, us bein' kin an' all," Matt said with a tone of respect in his voice.

"Make no mistake. Your brother is dangerous as hell, 'specially when he's mad. He's mad right now. But he ain't mean. He just don't take kindly to bein' lied to, cheated, or shot at," Joe reasoned.

"We'll be goin' now," Marcus said. "Mind if we take the rest of the coffee over to Seth? He probably wouldn't shoot nobody who brought him some coffee."

Joe smiled and told them to take the pot. Matt and Marcus walked away while Joe went back to his original position. Poor Delacourte, he thought, the man ain't got a chance now that them two's here. He checked his Sharps and settled down for a long wait.

On the other hill, the brothers joined forces without shooting at each other. Marcus and Matt made a lot of noise approaching and Seth recognized them before he started to take the slack up in the trigger of the Sharps. As with Joe before him, the brothers sat around and brought each other up to date. Seth, too, was pleased and more than a little proud of the way Sarah had handled herself with Brannon. Marcus and Matt wisely stayed away from the subject of the Seth-Sarah relationship. The brothers had fought over unguarded comments concerning the possibilities of Seth's love life before the war and they didn't want to get such a fight going so soon after getting together again. There would be time enough for that later.

"So, what's the plan with Delacourte?" Marcus asked.

"Now that you boys are here, I think we probably ought to start shooting the place to pieces. Those thin wood walls won't hold out the Sharps, even at this range. A couple of us could move in closer with the Henrys and wait for the men the other two smoke out of there with the Sharps."

"We only got one Henry," Matthew observed.

"There's another one in the scabbard on my saddle. It's back there under some brush by my horse. There's four or five boxes of shells in the saddlebags, too. If we can flush two or three of them out of there, I don't think we'll have to wait for darkness to take them. What do you think?"

Marcus and Matthew both agreed with Seth. Marcus said, "It's your show, Seth. Who's goin' to do what?"

"Marcus, I'd like you to stay on this side of the road and go as far forward as you can towards the house. I'll take the other Henry and move in from Joe's direction. Matt, you and Joe can start taking the house apart with the Sharps. I think that you can move about a hundred yards closer, too, since secrecy isn't important any longer. I'll get Joe to do the same. When we get a chance, Marcus, we'll rush the house."

"How much ammo you got for this here cannon?" Matt asked as he picked up the heavy rifle. "It's a sure 'nough killin' machine, ain't it?"

"There's about a hundred and fifty rounds for it, between what I've got here and what's back at the horses. I'll bring it up for you when I get the Henry. Fire about a hundred rounds of it at the house, no more than four shots a minute so the barrel doesn't get too hot and warp. Pay particular attention to the windows and the walls close to them when you start shooting. I figure that's where most of Delacourte's people will be crouched. I don't think I'd waste much ammunition on the roof. From closer in you aren't going to have a good angle for penetration, anyway."

Matthew nodded in understanding. Seth went to his saddle and returned carrying the Henry and the extra ammunition for the Sharps. "Wait twenty minutes before you start firing unless you see a target outside the house. That will give Marcus and me time to get into position. Good luck."

With that, Seth set out for Joe's position. Matthew looked at Marcus and smiled. "He's a pistol, ain't he? He's so cool it's almost scary. I wouldn't be Delacourte on a bet."

"Me neither, brother. Me neither," Marcus said as he wiped a spot of dust from the barrel of his Henry.

Chapter 14

The first round fired by Matthew from the big Sharps sent a four-inch sliver of wood flying across the room to strike Will Staden in the face, laying his cheek open to the bone. That shot was followed seven seconds later by another shot from an entirely different angle. That second shot struck no one, nor did any of the flying glass it produced. A slug ripped through the house every five to ten seconds thereafter. About five minutes into the barrage, Amos McCafferty, another of the ranch hands who had decided to fight for the brand, took a slug through the left knee that nearly tore his leg off. His scream could be heard clearly by both Joe and Matthew. Mercifully, Amos passed out quickly. Joe and Matt never slackened their rate of fire.

After ten minutes, Will Staden stood up screaming and ran for the door. A slug hit him and he died before he got halfway across the room. Seeking protection on at least three sides, Delacourte crawled into the stone fireplace and pulled the wreckage of a table across the opening. He felt or heard ricochets whine off the stones several times in the minutes that followed.

Beside Delacourte, only Cal Zimmer and the two deputies that had ridden with Delacourte to the ranch were still capable of putting up a fight. Then one of the deputies was hit in the arm, shattering it. That was too much for the remaining deputy, who picked up his Spencer and ran out of the room. Seth started tracking him as soon as he hit the door and put two slugs from the Henry into his chest before he cleared the porch. The deputy fell sprawling into the dirt, twitched once, and then laid still.

The firing from the hills stopped and both Marcus and Seth rushed for the house. Seth dropped the Henry and drew his Colt as he ran straight through the doorway and threw himself to the left. He could feel the wind from the slug fired by Cal Zimmer as it passed by his head. Seth fired twice at the moving man, missing both shots. He cursed under his breath and took the time as he laid there catching his breath to remove the two expended shells and thumbed two fresh cartridges into his pistol. He could detect no movement in the room.

Slowly Seth got to his feet and surveyed the wreckage of the house. Two hundred heavy caliber slugs had virtually destroyed the place. Furniture, bedding, and bodies laid scattered everywhere. Seth moved quickly through the three rooms examining the bodies. He found Amos McCafferty unconscious but alive. As he knelt to check McCafferty's wound, he heard Marcus shout.

"Behind you, Seth!"

Seth twisted as he let himself fall. He brought up his pistol and fired a split second before Cal Zimmer. Seth's shot caught Zimmer on the breastbone and lifted him onto his tiptoes. His lifeless body collapsed in a heap. Zimmer's shot threw splinters from the spot where it struck the doorway. Horton got unsteadily to his feet and reloaded.

"Thanks, Marcus. That was as close as I care to come to wearing wings."

"Was I you, I'd worry more about carryin' a pitchfork an' smellin' brimstone." The brothers laughed nervously, more from relief than from their feeble attempt at humor.

"I ain't seen anyone who looked too important here. Is Delacourte in this mess?" Marcus asked.

"No, he isn't, and that bothers me. Unless he snuck out of here last night, he should be around."

"All we got to do is burn the place. He'll either go up with it or come out quick."

Both men listened but could hear nothing. Delacourte sat like a statue in the fireplace, hardly daring even to breathe.

"Well, let's cart these bodies out of here first. Their mothers would appreciate it," Seth suggested.

"Maybe they would, but their fathers wouldn't. I'm bettin' that they met the mothers only once, briefly, cash on the barrelhead."

"Less talk and more work, Marcus. I have things to do."

"Yeah, I know. I met her in town."

Seth threw a table leg at Marcus, then dragged Mc-Cafferty and the wounded deputy well out into the yard. Quickly the two men pulled Brannon's body off the porch into the yard, then brought the remaining bodies out and placed them alongside Brannon's. Seth went to the barn to look for some torches.

"Last chance, Delacourte," Marcus shouted. "Come out or we fire the place." Delacourte remained where he was, unseen and silent.

Seth returned from the barn with two straw torches. He handed one to Marcus, then lit them both. The men threw the torches through smashed windows into different rooms.

The house was old and dry, and the open doors and shattered windows provided enough draft to encourage the flames to spread quickly. In a very short time, Marcus and Seth had to move back from the porch because of the heat. They heard Delacourte cry out seconds later.

"Don't shoot! I'm unarmed. I'm coming out!" he yelled.

"Come ahead. We'll keep you covered," Marcus yelled over the roar of the fire.

Delacourte appeared in the doorway a moment later and ran into the yard. His hair and clothing were smoking, and he was covered with soot. He threw himself on the ground and rolled in the dust to smother sparks that were threatening to burst into flames. He laid still for a few moments after that, catching his breath.

As Delacourte sat up, Marcus and Seth walked toward him, keeping him covered as they went. "So that's the big he-bear around here. He don't look so tough to me, Seth. How come it took you an' Joe more'n four months to put him out of business?"

"I guess you just had to be here to understand. Maybe I'm just getting old. I'm glad it's over though."

"It wouldn't be over if you two weren't holding those guns on me. Neither one of you has the guts to fight me face to face," Delacourte spat.

"Seems to me that he speaks awful mean for a fellow that had to send hired help after a pair of women," Marcus opined.

Seth holstered his pistol and unbuckled his gun belt. Carefully he handed it to Marcus. "Get up, Delacourte. I still owe you for Pepe and Ira Watkins."

As Delacourte stood up, Seth stepped in quickly and hit him squarely in the mouth with a vicious right that snapped Delacourte upright and then sent him onto the dirt on his back. "Hell, I owe it to me," Seth said as he stepped back. "Come on, Delacourte, get up. You aren't hurt that bad."

Delacourte rolled onto his belly and then got to his hands and knees. He shook his head to clear it, then spat out a tooth. Slowly he got to his feet. Crouching, he moved forward, fists clenched.

Seth moved in and hit Delacourte with two swift left jabs, then stepped back as Delacourte swung a roundhouse right that just missed his ear. Seth jabbed again at Delacourte's head and missed, then connected a solid right hook to his belly. Delacourte let out a groan as he bent at the waist and stepped back. Seth stepped in and threw a left at his head that missed and a right that caught Delacourte under the heart. Delacourte grunted and lashed out with an overhand right that connected with Seth's nose, bringing tears to his eyes. Off balance, Seth staggered back. Delacourte followed up with a vicious kick aimed for Seth's groin. Seth saw it coming and was able to turn in time, but he caught the blow on his right leg and hip.

Seth's vision dimmed from the explosion of pain, and he fell to the ground. Delacourte kicked him in the side, then jumped with both feet aimed at his chest. Seth rolled out of the way as Delacourte crashed to the ground next to him. Both men struggled to get to their feet. Delacourte made it first, stepped in, and hit Seth in the mouth with a left hook, knocking him back to the ground. Delacourte leaped on top of him,

The men rolled in the dirt, striking each other at every opportunity. Finally, Seth was able to knee Delacourte in the groin and roll away. Seth got to his feet slowly. Delacourte clutched himself with both hands and rolled onto his side. Seth waited until Delacourte was able to stand, then stepped in and hit him with a left and right to the belly. As Delacourte doubled over in pain, Seth grabbed Delacourte's hair with both hands and pulled his head down as he drove his right knee up into Delacourte's face. Delacourte's knees folded and he slipped to the ground. Seth held Delacourte's head up by the hair with his left hand and hit him twice in the face with his right. As he was preparing to hit him again, Seth felt Marcus grab his right arm.

"That's enough, Wolf. He can't feel it, anyway." Seth tried to break away, but Marcus held him firmly. "That's enough!" he said sternly. "It's over."

Gradually the need to kill subsided in Seth. He let go of Delacourte's hair and let him fall unconscious onto his face in the dust. Seth stood spread-legged and sucked air into his lungs. His head swam from his exertions, and he shook his head in a futile attempt to clear it. As his breathing slowed, Seth wiped the blood from his split lip and fingered his left eye, which was rapidly swelling shut.

"I must be a hell of a looking mess," he mumbled as he retrieved his gun belt from Marcus and put it back on. When he stooped to pick up his Henry, he nearly fell. "Hell of a way to treat a good rifle," he thought as he wiped dust from the action.

He walked back to Marcus and stood there with him as Joe and Matt came into the yard with the horses and dismounted. The shell of the house had collapsed into itself behind them. Suddenly Seth felt very weak.

"Riders comin'!" he heard Joe shout. The four men slowly separated and stood facing the approaching horsemen. There appeared to be a dozen or more moving rapidly towards them. As they got closer, Joe said, "Maybe my eyes is gettin' old, but I could swear there was a couple of women in the front of that bunch."

"You're right, Joe. I think that's Sarah and Marta up there in front," Marcus confirmed. "Is that old Rufus Pflugg with them?"

"I do believe you're right," Joe said. "Wonder what they're doin' way out here?"

"Just as long as we don't have to fight 'em," offered Seth. "I believe I've had enough of that for one day." The others laughed.

They were still laughing when the riders came to a halt in the yard. Marta and Sarah dismounted quickly. Sarah ran to Seth while Marta walked up to Joe.

"Seth! What happened to you?" She turned to Marcus. "Must he always do everything by himself? Couldn't you have helped him?" she cried.

"Don't blame him, Sarah. They all helped plenty. I sort of volunteered for this," Seth said softly as he touched his swollen face. "You should see the other guy." He smiled thinly and then winced from the pain.

"Oh, Seth," she cried as he slowly crumpled into the dust. Sarah knelt and cradled his head in her arms while the others took charge of Delacourte and the surviving men. "Thank God it's over," she said as she stroked his battered face.

Chapter 15

When Seth Horton awoke, he found himself in a real bed, complete with clean sheets and soft blankets. He opened one eye carefully and saw Sarah sitting next to him in a rocker. He tried opening the other eye and was rewarded by the sight of Joe and his brothers.

"He's back with us again," Marcus said. Everybody started talking at once.

"Hold it," Seth said weakly. "I can't follow what you're saying. How long have I been out?

"You've been in bed for almost a day," Sarah told him. "We brought you here, cleaned you up, and put you to bed. Doc Waterman told us you'd be fine after you got some rest."

"And I suppose it was you women who cleaned me up and put me here," Seth said as he pulled the covers higher.

"Of course. If it will make you feel any better, Marta and I kept our eyes closed while we were cleaning you up."

"You're outrageous, Sarah. Now suppose you get out of here while I get dressed. You did leave me some clothes, didn't you?

"The ones you didn't shred in the fight with Delacourte are on the trunk at the foot of the bed. You'll find some of father's shirts in the bureau. Help yourself to anything else you need. I'll go down and see if Marta needs any help with your breakfast." With that, Sarah left the room.

Seth sat up and swung his feet over the edge of the bed. Every muscle in his body was sore, and he groaned a little as he stood up. His brothers laughed as he hobbled around while he was getting dressed. "Instead of standing there laughing, suppose you tell me what I've missed. What happened to Delacourte?"

Marcus spoke for the group. "Well, it seems that after Matt an' I left for the Rafter T, Sarah and Marta looked up Rufus Pflugg an' told him about what happened with Brannon at her house an' later at the saloon with us. They also told him what we was up to at the Rafter T. Old Pflugg, he went an' called a town council meetin'. They decided it was time to quit feelin' sorry for themselves and get rid of Delacourte. What you saw ridin' in to the Rafter T was their posse. If we hadn't of cleaned out that mess, they would of." The rest of the men nodded in agreement.

"As for Delacourte, Pflugg an' his bunch brought him back here an' locked him in the grain room at the livery, seein' how you an' Joe here took their jail apart. The two wounded men are at Doc Waterman's. Pflugg sent word to Austin to send a judge. I believe they intend to give them a fair trial an' then hang 'em in front of the courthouse." Marcus stopped talking and then polled the others. "Is there anythin' important that I left out?"

"Can't think of nuthin'," Joe volunteered, "exceptin' maybe that Mayor Pflugg is comin' by this mornin'. Seems he wants to talk to you about somethin', Seth."

The other men smiled conspiratorially. Seth was tempted to ask them why the mayor wanted to talk to him but decided against it. It looked to him as though the brothers were setting him up for something, and he wasn't about to give them the satisfaction of walking into their trap. Seth finished dressing and walked over to the washstand. He saw a bruised face with a black eye looking back at him out of the mirror. The swelling was gone from the split lip, however, and Seth was beginning to feel like it hadn't been a mistake to get out of bed. He shaved as quickly as he could while the others talked about what else had happened in town since Joe and his brothers had left for the Rafter T fight.

Wiping the last of the lather from his face, Seth turned to the men. "Let's join the ladies. We need to decide what we're going to do about putting the ranch together again. Are you boys staying or heading off to seek your fortunes in the gold fields again?"

The five men walked downstairs as they talked. Seth learned that Joe had ridden to the Circle H after the fight and found three of the old Rafter T hands cleaning out the house. Although the kitchen was still unusable, the main house could be used for shelter until the headquarters could be rebuilt. Joe had retrieved the rest of the money from the fireplace and had purchased a quantity of lumber from Tad Beckley to rebuild the house and barns. Tad had said nothing about his broken locks or missing stores, and Joe had not brought the subject up, either.

In the kitchen, the five men and two women all sat around the table while Seth ate breakfast. The talk was mostly about how to repair the bullet holes Sarah had made in the floor during her run-in with Brannon. It seemed that everyone had some suggestion and each piece of advice was more outrageous than the last. By the time Seth was finished with his meal, he felt almost human again.

They were interrupted by a knock at the front door. Sarah left the group and opened the door to admit Rufus Pflugg. The rest of the group in the kitchen went into the parlor to greet the mayor.

"Glad to see you an' Jim are feelin' better, Seth," the mayor said as Horton shook his hand. "I'm real sorry that you all had to take care of Delacourte for us. Only it wasn't really Delacourte you was fightin'."

Seth looked at him in astonishment. "If it wasn't Delacourte we were fighting, who was it? I could have sworn it was Delacourte that gave me this eye." Seth winced as he touched his cheekbone.

"You fought the man, all right, but I got a wire from Austin this mornin' that says his name is really Jackson D. Devereaux. Seems he's a Union Army deserter."

"Of course!" Seth exclaimed. "I knew that I should've recognized the name when Myrna first said it. Jackson isn't all that common for a first name. So, there's a federal warrant out for him, too. Who gets to try him first?"

"The wire said for us to go ahead an' they'll try whatever's left. I doubt that the government will have any interest in tryin' a dead man, though."

Mayor Pflugg shifted his feet and cleared his throat. "What I really come for this mornin', Seth, was to talk to you. With Ira bein' gone an' us in bad need of some law around here, the town council and I got together an' voted to offer you the job. I hope you'll accept it. We need you for the job."

Seth was caught totally unprepared. Looking around at others grinning back at him, it dawned on him that this was the conspiracy he had sensed upstairs. Once the shock wore off, he turned back to the mayor.

"I'm honored, Mister Mayor, but I can't accept your offer. You need stability in the job and an honest man to fill it. The truth of the matter is that in a few days, I'll be leaving."

It was the others' turn to be shocked. Sarah was the first to speak out.

"Oh, Seth, you can't! You just can't leave now! Why?"

Seth turned to her. "Sarah, I'm going to Kansas. I never got out of the Army. I know I don't look like it, but I was sent here to recuperate from my injuries and then report to Fort Riley to command the cavalry regiment. Now that my brothers are back to keep the ranch going, there's nothing left to hold me here."

"Nothing left to hold you here? Do you mean ... don't I ...," Sarah stammered as tears gathered in her eyes.

"Nothing, that is, provided that you'll come with me, Sarah. A commanding officer needs a lady."

"Do you mean what I think you mean? If you do, Seth Horton, you'll have to say it right here in front of God and everybody!" Sarah exclaimed.

"Very well." Seth cleared his throat. "Sarah, I love you and want you for my wife. Will you marry me?"

Seth was very nearly knocked to the floor as Sarah threw herself into his arms. "It certainly took you long enough. Of course I will." Then she kissed him soundly.

After a few moments, the sound of applause brought them back to reality. Embarrassed, they broke off their embrace. Everybody began talking and congratulating the happy couple.

Finally, Seth spoke. "Mister Mayor, we still haven't settled the problem of selecting a lawman. If you'd take the advice of a Yankee cavalry colonel, I suggest you make Matthew here your sheriff. I don't think you'll find a better man."

"That sounds good to me," the mayor said. "How about it, Matthew? Will you take the job?"

Matt scratched his head for a moment and then looked up. "Why not?" he said. "I'd kinda like to do that. It'll beat the hell outta chasin' cows. If you want me, I guess I'm your man, Mister Mayor."

Just then, Lefty from the livery ran up onto the porch and said breathlessly, "Rufus, you better come quick. I went to take some food to the prisoner like you said an' found poor Clarence in the grain room instead of Delacourte. The door was open an' Delacourte's long gone. Looks like he broke Clarence's neck an' then stole one of my horses an' rode out. No tellin' how long he's been gone. Clarence went on guard at midnight an' I was goin' to keep an eye on things durin' the day."

Mayor Pflugg turned to Matthew. "Sheriff, here's your first case. What are you goin' to do about it?"

"Guess I'll go take a look." He walked to the hall tree and retrieved his gun belt and hat and set off for the livery with Lefty close behind. Pflugg turned back to Seth. "Sorry to break this up, but I have to get back. We've got a lot of work to do puttin' the town back together after your fight with Delacourte, or Devereaux, or whatever his name is. Good luck to you, Seth, and to you, too, Sarah."

"Thank you, Mayor. We appreciate it," Seth responded as he went with Pflugg to the door. "I'm sure we'll see you again before we leave." The two men shook hands and Pflugg set off for the center of town.

Marcus, James, and Joe joined Seth on the porch. "You leavin' right away?" Marcus asked.

"We'll stay until I heal up a bit. I don't want to walk into a new command looking like this. Besides, I'm sure that Sarah would prefer to be married here. I'll talk to her, but I think that we'll be leaving in a week or two."

"Seems a shame to see you go so soon," Jim offered. "But I expect you'll be back from time to time. You're always welcome at the ranch, you know, as a brother and as a partner."

Sarah and Marta joined the men on the porch. "I wonder where Delacourte is?" Marta said. "He's such an evil man!"

"I don't know, Marta," Seth said, "but you can bet that a man like him will show up again. I can't help feeling that I should have killed him when I had the chance. If I had, poor Clarence would still be alive."

"Don't blame yourself for that, Seth Horton," Sarah scolded. "You had no way of knowing it would turn out this way."

"You're probably right," Seth said as he put his arm around Sarah, "but I've got a feeling that I'll have to fight Delacourte again." Slowly they followed the others into the house.

Two hundred yards away, Delacourte centered the sights of his Springfield rifle on Seth Horton's back.

He took up the slack in the trigger and squeezed off his shot. The hammer fell with authority, striking the percussion cap positioned beneath it. There was a loud "click."

Misfire! Delacourte swore bitterly and dug into this pocket for a new percussion cap. By the time he had replaced the defective one, the front door closed and the opportunity was lost forever.

Delacourte threw down the rifle in disgust, then walked back to where he had hidden the horse he had stolen from the livery. "There'll be a next time, Horton, you can bet on it," he muttered under his breath. "Relax. Forget about me. One day I'll find you again and then you'll die."

He mounted the horse and headed south toward Mexico and sanctuary from the law.

~ The End ~

Colonel R.C. Hartjen joined the Army at age 17 and was commissioned six years later. He has commanded an Armored Cavalry troop in Germany, an Airborne Cavalry troop in Viet Nam, and a tank battalion in the United States.

He holds an earned doctorate in counseling psychology and is a graduate of the US Army War College. Although he has written a number of articles and monographs for military publication, this is first novel.

Colonel Hartjen is retired and makes his home in Leavenworth, Kansas along with his wife, Helen, and their devoted yellow Labrador, Annie.